Love and Life
Behind the Purdah

Love and Life Behind the Purdah

Cornelia Sorabji

MINT EDITIONS

Love and Life Behind the Purdah was first published in 1901.

This edition published by Mint Editions 2021.

ISBN 9781513280141 | E-ISBN 9781513285160

Published by Mint Editions®
 MINT
EDITIONS
minteditionbooks.com

Publishing Director: Jennifer Newens
Design & Production: Rachel Lopez Metzger
Project Manger: Micaela Clark
Typesetting: Westchester Publishing Services

Contents

A Letter from Lord Hobhouse to the Author   9

The Pestilence at Noonday   13

Love and Life   37

Love and Death   46

Urmi   52

Greater Love   56

Behind the Purdah   64

Malappa   75

A Living Sacrifice   78

The Fire is Quenched!   84

Achthar   93

Pundit-je   99

This collection of Indian stories will be found both interesting and suggestive.

They are charmingly told, they are full of incident, and they exhibit to us from the inside, as it were, customs and ways of living and of thinking which we usually contemplate from the outside only, and which we are apt to consider and appraise through the mists of our own European prejudices. → assumptions

The writer is herself an Indian, and one whose strength of character and talent have enabled her to face the difficulties of a University education, and to pass successfully the examinations which, in the case of a male student, would qualify him to practise at the Indian Bar.

The aim and ambition of Miss Sorabji's life has been to benefit and to serve her countrywomen, and in these pages will be found evidences of her deep sympathy and affection for them.

Her stories set before us, in the most attractive way, the tender, faithful, meek, and lowly character of the Indian woman, combined as it so often is with a quiet persistence and strength, and with an unselfishness which amounts to self-sacrifice.

Perhaps in these days of stress and strain, of activity and competition, a peculiar interest may be found in contemplating lives spent in the strict privacy of the purdah, under the iron discipline of custom, and in observing, with reverence and admiration, the way in which the virtues of patience, charity, self-forgetfulness, and devotion to duty, flourish in this silent and secluded world.

It is true that in these stories heroic actions are often performed from mistaken motives and through superstitious fears, but we may certainly hope and believe, that, like as suttee has disappeared before the march of Christianity and of civilization, so other trials peculiar to the lives of Indian women may gradually soften and pass away.

HARIOT DUFFERIN and AVA

A Letter from Lord Hobhouse
to the Author

Dear Miss Sorabji,—I have to thank you for allowing me to read in quiet the tales of Indian life which you have composed. My own connection with India was not such as to bring me into personal contact with those social and domestic affairs of which you treat. I resided there not longer than five years. My time and energies were fully occupied with office work. I learned not a word of any of the vernacular languages, and only a few expressions of the more artificial *lingua franca* of the educated classes. Even in this Hindustani I rarely trusted myself to speak except to give directions to my own servants. A man so situated cannot get any but the most superficial notions of the multitudes around him.

The physical features of a portion of the vast country I traversed; the external appearance of portions of its multifarious populations; brief occasions of friendly intercourse with men of high rank and cultivated minds with whom my official position brought me into acquaintance; an examination here and there into the working of some law among the people,—such alone were my opportunities of knowledge at first-hand. At second-hand, I, like everybody else who sees much of the administrative class, heard many of their ideas from various points of view and under different circumstances. After my return it became my duty to pay attention to Indian lawsuits coming before the king in council; and from them I have got some partial, incomplete, and hasty glimpses into the interior of Indian villages and domestic life. Owing to these circumstances it is possible that an Indian story, such as you tell, may convey a more vivid impression, perhaps a truer one, to me than to one who has never been in India at all. But I am very far indeed from being qualified to pass any judgment on your book as a work of art, or to comment on it as you invite me to do. To express opinions of its fidelity to the Indian life which I have not seen, would be presumptuous; and if I were to attempt it, not only would you yourself detect the imposture, but any other reader would soon find out which of us was writing with knowledge and which without.

There is, however, one subject of considerable importance which has been much impressed on me by my experience in Indian litigation; and that is the position of the Indian woman who is of sufficiently high rank to be a *parda-nashin*. I am not now speaking of the social side of the seclusion of women. It is obvious to any observer what a bar it presents to social intercourse, and how profoundly impediments to social intercourse weaken the political structure of a country. But as with the cognate institutions of caste, of village communities, or of ancestor-worship, so with these ideas of what is due to the dignity of women—long custom has woven them into the very fabric of Indian society. It may be, probably is, the case that they prevent the gradual fusion of tribes, castes, communities, families, or other limited divisions of mankind, into the higher order of a nation; but among the individuals of these limited divisions they form a social cement of the strongest conservative force. Not only do they preserve peace and order, but, unless my impressions are much mistaken, they meet some social needs in easier fashion than is found possible in the more vigorous national life of Western Europe. For instances, I should mention the settlement of petty disputes and the support of the indigent. If it were possible to take away these social sanctions suddenly, or even rapidly, the result would be chaos, some frightful disruptions and convulsions. The traditions of the multitudinous social aggregates in India, all strengthened and endeared to them by a halo of religion, are—or so at least it seems to one who is not of them—to each the world in which they live and move and have their being, socially keeping each in their places, just as the insensible force of gravitation and the insensible pressure of the atmosphere do physically for all of us. They supply the support and guidance of life, all that is done for us by kings, parliaments, law-courts, churches, schools, and, in addition, by the still more constant and powerful, though subtle and undefined, influence of public opinion, the desire to stand well with our families, friends, and neighbours. Such safeguards of conduct cannot be beneficially removed or weakened except by some extremely slow and gradual process of thought, by which broader and more elastic principles of social obligation may be substituted for narrower rules, giving as much support with greater freedom of movement. That is a matter for the distant future and for infinite incalculable workings of the human spirit.

Nevertheless, with all my respect for the reign of custom and tradition, and with full perception of the danger of rude interference with the delicate tissues of family life and personal feelings, it is consistent to advocate plans by which their inconvenient consequences may be lessened. The inconveniences attending on the seclusion of an Indian lady when she has dealings with the outer world are constantly coming to the surface. A large number of ladies own property, and some are owners of large and important properties. They cannot escape from the responsibilities of ownership, nor can they rightly perform the duties or receive the benefits attaching to it, without entering into legal relations with the world outside. The Hindu and Mohammedan laws are neither of them unfavourable to women as regards the enjoyment of property; indeed, both of them are much more favourable than our English common law, whose rigour against the female sex has only within the last few years been mitigated by statute. But behind the law there is the custom which makes it dishonourable for Indian ladies to "appear before" any male person except within a limited range of their own family. This interposes serious difficulties in their dealing with property. The effect is to prohibit free and unrestrained conversation between the lady and a male outsider. And as every professional lawyer is of the male sex, communication between the lady and her legal adviser is much impeded. *A fortiori*, it is so with other persons who have business with her. Talking with a person behind a curtain is a very different thing from talking face to face. Indeed it is not always certain that the man outside has got hold of the right woman inside. She requires identification by someone who has the right to be inside, and fraudulent personations are not unknown. It may be that the males of the family are the very persons about whose encroachments the lady wants advice—a point which is illustrated by one of your present sketches.

This is a mere outline of the case, which to be accurate would require both qualification and supplement; but it is true enough to warrant the assertion that the rights which are clearly conferred on Indian women by law are subject to large practical drawbacks by the practice of secluding ladies. To show the extent and importance of these drawbacks, it is only necessary to cite a well-known rule of law established in Indian courts. Everyone who comes to enforce a contract against a parda-nashin finds that the ordinary presumptions of law are inverted to his disadvantage. Instead of presuming that the legal owners of property know what they are about when they deal with it, he who deals with a parda-nashin has to prove that the transaction was explained to and understood by her. Such proof is, under the circumstances indicated, often difficult; and I fully believe that honest claims are often defeated in that way. Protective rules of this kind mean that those who deal with the protected person must take special precautions, and that again means that bargains made by the protected persons are harder than those made by free people. Every litigation in which parda-nashins are concerned disclose difficulties of this kind, and others on which this is not the place to enlarge.

It is true that these disabilities could not be got rid of without greater encroachment on the practice of seclusion than Indian sentiment could accept, possibly greater than would be good for Indian families; but as regards their visibly mischievous effects, these might be substantially abated without any encroachment at all. What is wanted is that parda-nashin ladies should have unrestricted access to persons versed in legal affairs. This could be done if such persons were ladies like themselves. I feel sure that if parda-nashin owners of property could be visited by ladies competent to understand their cases, to prepare them for advice, or perhaps to advise on them at first-hand; to take evidence direct from them when required for judicial purposes, to explain documents, to obtain their execution—in short, to do things face to face which are now done through a veil—they would own those properties more fully, in much nearer accordance with the provisions of the law, and with beneficial results both to themselves and to all who have honest dealings with them. Your efforts in this direction have now become known to many, and are becoming more known. Such a movement must have very small beginnings, but if sound in principle, as you and I believe, it must surely extend itself. On its extent, and the precise mode of its working, it is premature to speculate; for this must be regulated by social needs and by men's appreciation of its value. You, at any rate, are doing what you can to promote it—partly by holding up phases of Indian society to view, mainly by offering in your own person an instance of a lady competent to act as a "man of business" if only she can obtain the requisite position and the requisite recognition of her usefulness. And so may you prosper.

You are quite welcome to publish this letter if you think it likely to be of use.

I am, faithfully yours,
HOBHOUSE

THE PESTILENCE AT NOONDAY

I

BUT YOU WILL FORGET ME, my lord!"

"Yes! 'tis not unlikely," was the response. "I shall have many things to interest me: knowledge to acquire, the world to sample, a name to make. How, then, will there be room for thought of women, and petting, and suchlike? But when I am tired of it all I'll come back to this forgotten little spot, and I'll find you just the same, sitting here among the lotuses and marigolds, and with a heart just as full of love for me as it is now—rather fuller, perhaps, with the enforced repression!"

"Oh, my lord, how unkind you are! I've spoiled you!"

"Have you indeed? Who would be the more unhappy, you or I, did my father wed me to the wealthy Tara? Now listen. Seriously, Sita, you must drop this nonsense. I am sorry that I let them educate you. It has given you notions which patch clumsily on to the heritage of traditions into which you were born. Remember you are still a Hindu wife, however glibly your tongue may adapt itself to foreign languages. And remember what that means. When you rode the 'marriage' horse beside me (how many years ago was that?), or, even later, when you trod the seven steps round the sacred fire, 'twas not because I loved you, or you loved me. It was partly, as you know, because the astrologers gave the word, and partly because your dowry was sufficiently attractive. True it is that I fought your battles for you, Sita, when we were children together, playing in the great courtyard at our *gillie-dandu* or our *ātia pātiā;* and I won't deny that I have been very kind to you, letting them teach you most of the things I learnt myself, and saving you from household drudgeries. And I have even let you call me by my name, and raise your eyes in my presence, and dine, sitting by my side (think of that!), and I daresay you've boasted of all this to the women at the well, of a morning. But I warn you, Sita, set not too much store by these indulgences. They are indicative of nothing save, perhaps, of my own superiority to trifles." (Sita stole a look at him. No! he was quite serious.)

"There is, remember, a habit of loving, and it includes in its generous scope all who come within physical range of its influence—all accustomed daily objects. Think of all that that may mean, Sita, in the long years when you no longer form an item in my immediate horizon. Think of it, and perhaps that will cure you of expecting too much. . . Yes! the gods and fate have created you for my convenience and ministration; the only dignity which you can ever acquire will be incidental. Hitherto you have failed me, and were I to die to-morrow, who is there to raise the supplicatory censer beside the pyre?

"Be thankful, little Sita, for what of affection and indulgence you have been allowed, and while I am away you will best please me by being a good daughter to my old father. *He* dotes on you, you know, and—well, I won't promise, but give me your ear, Sita; *if* you should send me word that I need not fear about the funeral pyre—you understand?—why, I may hurry home in a year or so—who knows?"

They stood by a little pond of lotuses—the man and woman; both strong, handsome young creatures, developed wholesomely, mind and body. The girl, in her clinging white and green draperies, seemed herself but a human rendering of the delicate yet stately flower, as it floated in its dainty purity on the close surface of graceful green leaves. And the man seemed to be noting this with an air of satisfied proprietorship through his half-shut, sleepy eyelids. She had been a bit playful to begin with, and had even ventured a jeer or two and a saucy glance with her handsome black eyes; but, as the unimpassioned homily proceeded she drew away, hurt and doubtful, and listened with drooping head.

There was now a moment's silence. An ugly toad dared a clumsy leap over the divine lotus, and Het Ram threw a stone at him. The sound roused Sita; she drew herself up to her full height, and seemed about to speak; but changing her mind, she walked rapidly away.

"Sita!" called her husband; but for once no little caressing creature came to rub a gentle cheek against his extended hand.

II

IT IS NINE YEARS SINCE the scene by the lotus bed. The hour is again that of the short Indian twilight. The little silver bell tinkles at a wayside shrine, calling the labouring man to propitiate the idol for the carelessness and detected dishonesties of his day's labours, and goodly Hindus, men and women, stream down the busy thoroughfare, responsive to the call. The street presented a whole spectrum of exquisite colour. There were the graceful draperies of the women, and the brilliant turbans of the men—for the sterner sex is, in India, allowed the indulgence of primitive tastes for the attractive in dress; and, indeed, to the seeing eye, the little procession was inarticulate history. That sharp-eyed, slightly-built man with the curious close-fitting turban, terminating in a seeming bottomless crown, is by caste and profession a *bania*, or money-lender; he probably comes from Kathiawad, and the well-worn books under his left arm contain, I doubt not, matter sufficiently explanatory of the anxious look on his unabsolved countenance.

With this other devotee, humorous, kindly, old, one wishes better acquaintance.

On his forehead he bears an open triangle and a large black dot—the mark significant of the god to whom he has allotted himself, the classic Vishnu; and he divides his attention between a pair of old steel scissors and a pair of new red shoes, which last he carries carefully under a protecting left arm. The white dust is not unpleasing to his toes, and, as for the shoes, they are no addition to the dignity of old Narain the tailor, than whom the town holds no more respected citizen.

Beside him walks a hybrid production, a creature evidently of the very new school. His large, flat, red turban with its golden fringe is his one concession to his caste. For the rest, he creaks aloud in cheap patent leather shoes and dubious white socks—ineffectual covering for a gratuitous display of muscleless leg, surmounted by folds of loose white drapery and a rusty black coat. He is discussing with old Narain the chance of escape for the city from the dread disease, news of which is brought from infected towns by fear-stricken refugees. But his pompous periods are suspended for remark on the slender, gracefully clad figure of a woman, who, avoiding the crush, hugs the shop-fronts, hurrying swiftly forward to anticipate the inrush at the little temple.

"You know Sita?" he says complacently to his companion, "Sita of the house of Nagarkar, the old pundit? In a week or so she will be my bride. There are no prouder souls on this incarnation than the girl and her father: but they will yet be suppliant to me. I shall not curse this sickness if it humbles them—not but that Sita will be worth the price I pay,"—he added generously. "She will be a great help to me over my new paper. 'Tis well to educate girls sometimes, it makes them marketable."

Bhikku the oilman jostled him at this moment. He was clad in a slight garment wound about his loins; of distinctive headdress he was innocent, but his shining personality advertised his calling with sufficient emphasis; and he bore, pendent, a small vessel full of the sweet oil of the country. A judicious swing deposited a full pice-worth on the brand-new patent leather.

"Hi, Master Gopal!" exclaimed the knave, in well-simulated sullen resentment, "you know how to write essays on the rights of the poor, and the wrong done us by the Government with its taxes and assessments; but what of the champion of the poor himself, who robs the poor man of his oil, and the god of his offering?"

"Insolent son of a pig!" retorted Gopal, who had already been instant with curses and bitterness, "what of my new shoes?"

But a general laugh forced upon his wounded vanity the need of some display, and, "There!" he added, "you are not worth consideration; replace your oil, and buy yourself some manners!"

Bhikku's eyes dilated at sight of the rupee, and clutching it eagerly he turned aside to test it on the pavement—gratitude came not but in the wake of an assuring ring. Then, "Protector of the poor," he yelled after the retreating figure, "may the thread of your life continue unending; 'tis Bhikku the oilman who prays it. . . And," he added in a lower tone to the knot of loiterers who had backed him, "may Bhikku often bespatter your infidelclad feet, in the presence of such true worshippers of the gods as these my brethren!"

Indeed, so elated was he by the success of his device, that he would willingly have scattered largess to the extent of three whole pice—had he not feared that 'twould be accepted!

Sita has now reached the little shrine. 'Tis a small stone pavilion, to which a few worn steps give access. The idol is—as man has made him; and sits smiling blandly through more than one coating of oil and green paint. Over his head is an umbrella, the emblem of sovereignty; a quiver of arrows hangs at his back; in one hand he holds his bow of destruction, and in the other a flower of the living lotus, as who should say, "I slay, and I make alive."

Sita, his wife, once sat by his side, but in a fit of jealousy at her transcendent beauty he killed her, say the priests, one stormy night, with his great bow and arrow, and a shred of protecting veil, with a fragment of broken arm, emphasised the story, as it filtered down to generations yet unborn.

Yet, clearly, his devotees were not as other religionists were, or even as some mere sensationalists, seeking to realise Ram Chandra's graphic omnipotence by means of gigantic efforts after magnificence and ceremony—for they worshipped quietly enough—the humblest of them himself* approaching the god with his simple offering, unattended by acolyte or mace-bearer, or any pomp and circumstance of prayer. At most, on festal days, the blind priest from beneath the pipal tree would be requisitioned in attendance—to beat, with upturned face and wriggling body, a wild tattoo on an ill-shapen and tuneless drum.

To-day, however, Ram Chandra was in mufti, so Sita found her way, unimpeded into the silence of the presence-chamber, and dropped at the petrified feet of the idol her small offering—a handful of yellow marigolds and some beauteous white lotus flowers. Then she retreated, and looked at the smug, complacent creature with some scorn. "You *are* ugly," she said. "Is it to propitiate you that I continue my daily sacrifice? I certainly do not love you. And you have done nought for me these nine long years. Perhaps you have not the power even to hurt me. Perhaps you are just a poor dead block of stone, after all—just that, and nothing more!"

But the people were approaching, so she hastened to add her usual orison. "Good luck to my dear husband, and oh! a swift return!"

Then, drawing her veil closer about her, she turned and sped back the way she had come.

The door into the little courtyard creaked painfully as she helped it open, and there was a sad look of poverty and ill-fought decay about the once handsome house. The old carvings along the wood balcony were chipped and casual; no longer did the serpent-headed sport in wanton freedom with apocryphal nymphs, and the famous monkeys leered in the most sinister of split mouths at the great Vishnu and Lakshmi, whom erstwhile they had worshipped with abject dejection, in the sanctified company of Hanuman the divine. While, apart from artistic effect, what of the safety of those great tottering columns?

In the broad verandah on a large wooden swing, hanging by rusty iron chains from the beams overhead, sat a venerable old man, clean-shaven, head and face, but for a small wisp of thin grey hair, which, grown in the centre of his head, was gathered into a single long-looped knot, and bobbed against his back in perfect accord with the motion of the board. Curled close beside him, the old man's lean right arm keeping him in steady safety, was a poor wee child, his face too keenly intelligent and his eyes too lustrous for health.

You would have thought he was but six years in age, but he had been in this sad world about four years longer. His eyes brightened at sight of his mother. "Mother," he said, "come and swing—see! there's room for you." But the old pundit stopped the intended game.

"Nay, mother of Rama!" he said, "I would speak with thee. Give to the care of the trusty Mukti this thy son, and come thou with me to the lotus pond."

Sita bent her head in grave acquiescence, and summoning the nurse, had soon overtaken the stately-stepping pundit.

"What is it, father?" she asked, her hand in his. "What ails thee—the day's sunset?"

"Nay!" he made answer; "by the lotus bed will I speak."

Sita helped him mount the little mound overlooking the still water and the eternal flowers, and, throwing down a square of gay Indian carpet to protect the aged limbs against the early dew, "Now," she said, expectant.

"My child," said the sage, "in the holy book is there all wisdom; yet not even much reading and study of the word teaches one when and of whom the gods may demand vengeance. Whether we ourselves, you and I, Sita, or whether our ancestors have sinned, how can I tell, whence discover? But this I do know, that, unless the gods relent, some fearful calamity awaits us. The oracles have never lied to me. Now, child of my heart, hear me; but hear the worse alternative first. Thou knowest that there is but a handful of rupees in the jar, buried over against the Buddha column. 'Tis true that, as a Brahmin, my demand for money would bring a special blessing to Lalluchand, that godless son of the stone-bleeding banker, or to any of those ill-begotten dogs of usurers. But ever since the old Krishnaram, the ancestor of your son, got the rich grant of land from the grateful but wily Sivaji (never mind that story now, you know it), no sleek bania has written our honoured names in his dishonest account books—nor shall he do so now! And 'tis thou must help me, Sita. Gopal of the Samachar seeks thy hand in marriage; he promises gifts, unusually generous. Thou hast for two years been accounted a widow. Have we not waited nine long years for some sign of life from thy husband? That the demon of the sea has prepared him for his next incarnation seems certain, beyond a doubt. Why shouldst thou wear thy young eyes with watching down the avenue of all the weary years, for a wanderer who will never come? Gopal is clever; you will have many tastes in common. For thy son's sake, Sita, consent to this. Gopal is impatient (and I blame him not),—was here urging me, just after thou didst leave this evening for the temple, light of my eyes. . . For thy boy's sake," he repeated, as the girl still spoke not.

Then she lifted to him a face almost stern with resolution. "No, father, not yet—I cannot. *For my husband's sake* I remain unmarried, till he comes to claim me. If he be dead (and of this I must have proof), then—why, then, what matters it to me what life I lead, whether as Gopal's wife or another's? Yet, I tell you, father, I like not this new notion of re-marriage. Your grandparents would have deemed it sin. . . But he is not dead, I know; and there *is* a way other than the one through Gopal's courtyard. Of what avail is all that you have let me learn, all the Sanskrit and English and other things, an I am less able to help myself than the woman who grinds the corn for our daily bread? I will seek my old teacher; she will surely show me how to make use of my learning."

The old man looked at her in admiration. "Thou wert ever quick-witted, Sita. But the plan is too untried to praise—just yet. Meantime, now that thou hast heard the worse alternative, and heard it with courage, listen to the possible escape. Dost thou remember my talk of Symonds sahib, the planter on the—estate? Sociable he was, and open-handed, learned also in the ways and language of our people, and *river-hearted*, ever kind to those in distress. But he was reckless and extravagant, and the women of his acquaintance were more exacting than the greediest idol. Soon his debts became matter for scandal in the department, and he came to me. We had enough and to spare then: 'twas many years agone, now, Sita—you would not remember—and he was an Englishman, and had been good to me. 'Twas not like lending money to the close-fisted bania—so—well! I hold a bond for 10,000 rupees. He meant well by me, for his bankers have till lately sent me the interest regularly. 'Tis true 'twas but a nominal rate, but that was at my own desire. *I* would not be a bania, putting out money to be doubled in my friend's houses! But what I can't understand is the fact that the auguries are not more favourable! For, look you, he is now in this neighbourhood, and—he is an English gentleman. If I go to him and say, 'Sir, I have not pressed my bond these many years, but we are in trouble; the little Sita whom you saw as a child, and her boy, and I. . . and, though I am ashamed to ask it, we want the money, now.' . . . or, perhaps my voice will fail me, ere I've said a thing, but he will understand, and will take my hand, and say, 'My friend, why did you not come to me earlier, or press for the money through my bankers? Would you not have me come to you in my trouble?—nay, did I not come?' And, I shall be ashamed for another cause—for this indeed, that I am so poor a creature that to beg a kindness of my friend is gall to me. And I shall weep, but I'll be happy too, in that he will have saved you, Sita, and the boy. . . and, I will come to you, with my hand tightly clasped on that little cheque of his—a small piece of paper, Sita, why, the wind, even on a still day, would bear it away like a feather! but it will mean freedom for us, and life and health to the boy. . . And we shall journey, we three, to the far hills where the air is pure, and where no dragon of disease can stalk in our wake. But, Sita! Sita! Sita! tell me, *why* were the auguries inauspicious? Is it that I may never meet him? But *you* could claim the money? The boy would still be saved. What matters about me? the thread of my life is nearly run out." . . . Then, suddenly, "I will go to him to-morrow, Sita; we shall cheat the Fates, *yet!*"

He rose with some of his old energy, and was indeed quite cheerful over the simple evening meal, recalling stories of his own dear planter sahib, and acquiring fresh confidence from his reminiscences. . .

"Why, you look ten years younger, my father!" said Sita, as in the freshness of the early morning she equipped him for his journey, binding his small bundle about his shoulders, and herself placing the staff in his well-knit hand.

"You will deduct a second decade on my return," he chuckled.

But the gate creaked ominously behind him.

III

"THERE IS REALLY NOTHING MORE luxurious than tent-life in India." It was an Englishwoman who spoke her thoughts aloud, and she spoke in a brisk cheery voice. She seemed about forty years or thereabouts; the eyes were small and round and kindly, and the sunburnt face beamed health and benevolence. She lay in a low deck-chair, under the flap of a comfortable Jubbalpore tent. "How *am* I to make them believe at home that here, a hundred miles from civilization, I have—all this?' And she inspected her canvas home with much satisfaction. Small shelves of attractive books hung against the walls of the tent. In one corner stood a table, littered with the nameless requisites of a lady's letter-writing. Soft Persian rugs wooed one's feet. A table laid with spotless linen and glittering silver promised speedy pacification to clamorous appetites. Easy-chairs and soft cushions offered repose to tired limbs. She rose with a sigh of content and walked to the tent door. The little encampment gleamed white in the early sunlight. "I wish they'd come," she said. And, as though her wish were electric, the clatter of horses' hoofs came to her on the wind.

At a casual glance these men might have served, at an imperial exhibition of human beings, as typical of the Anglo-Indian. The routine of officialism, the strict application of codes with the one and the habit of ruling with the other, seemed to have robbed their faces of much individuality. They were no longer John Caldecott and Henry Symonds— they were the trusted commissioner and the successful tea-planter. The characteristics of the type, however, were sufficiently forcible: hard, stern faces, browned with exposure to sun and wind; the light active frame of men whose lives had been spent in the country of sport; and the careless good humour of the exile in the company of boon companions. But closer observation revealed differences. Henry Symonds had squandered all the good material with which life had endowed him. He had wasted his substance—not exactly in the riotous living of the prodigal, but in brainless extravagances, usually wild bids for popularity. He had a generous heart and an instinctive dread of giving pain, but he allowed an entire severance between wit and sentiment, and, as a result, his generosity was rarely well-placed; while the dislike of pain had grown to a curiously sensual and selfish aestheticism.

The chief human being to be saved from pain was himself. Yet he was excellent company, could tell a good story and sing a rollicking song, was invaluable at private theatricals, and had even written a stray novel or two. Sinister tales were afloat, of not altogether justifiable attempts to readjust the inactivities of his banking account; but those stern lines about the mouth belied the rumours.

His friends did not reflect that the trend of the workaday mill may have been a more peremptory force in his life than any effort of his own weak nature.

However, here he was—a godsend in the desert, and in three short months John Caldecott would be waving a white handkerchief to the P. and O. boat which carried his friend to an evening of quiet in the Devonshire village where he meant to make his home.

"Here you are, you hunters," said cheery Mrs. Caldecott. "You must defer baths till after breakfast. If you've not brought the proverbial hunger home with you, it's because I've usurped the craving."

Food was not hard to procure in this district. The eggs and milk of the outlying villages were a great improvement on the dwarfed and diluted productions of the towns; while of flesh they had an assortment varied by each fresh expedition of the sportsmen. It is true that, in deference to the prejudices of their Hindu neighbours in these ignorant wilds, they forbore from the sacred cow, but tinned substitutes offered sufficient opportunity for homage to British instincts. And indeed the encampment had nought culinary of which to complain.

Conversation, as is not uncommon in India, was mostly of the pig-sticking and polo type, and the men continued, after breakfast, to exchange experiences over their cigars, while Mrs. Caldecott busied herself at her writing-table. Presently she looked round. "I was quite forgetting," she said, "that there is a queer old man waiting in the office-tent, to see the planter sahib. He is a most picturesque creature, with a certain quiet dignity in his face and bearing. He was carrying his own bundles, and looked quite poor; but there was something about him which made me feel almost shamefaced when they sent him to the office instead of showing him in here. Could you go and see him at once, Mr. Symonds? It seems not right to keep him waiting any longer."

Mr. Symonds rose at once, and his friend promised to follow in a minute, to see to a stray official letter or so.

"Oh, Shastri, my good friend, greeting!" said the ever-ready Henry. "It is close upon—how many years since I saw you? And now tell me of the small girl, and that boy of yours." . . . So he rattled on in his old familiar way.

"He's just the same," said the poor old man to himself; and, drawing on the thought for courage, he produced the bond, and made his request. . .

When Mr. Caldecott reached the tent his friend was laughing a hard laugh as he tore up a stamped document; and a shrunken little man was cowering opposite him, with a face that was almost ashen.

"Hallo, Symonds! What's the row? Is the wife's prince a badmaash?"

"Oh, no! he's only a creditor claiming ten thousand rupees, *and more*—that's all! That's the bond!" and he pointed to the torn fragments in the waste-paper basket.

Caldecott shook his head unbelievingly. "You were always an actor, Symonds," he said, "and that was really a fine scene. Put it into your next play; 'twill be a variation on the immortal Shylock. . . But, I say, that man *does* look ill. What is the matter? Will he have a peg?"

"Not he!" said Symonds; "and not even water, *from us*. He's a Brahmin of the Brahmins. Why, I remember a journey he made in my company one hot, thirsty day, when his respect for his mother, the cow, nearly parched his throat eternally. The only place where water was procurable was in the vicinity of the shambles, and, 'I can't drink here,' he said. . . Come, Shastri, don't take on so. That paper would have made no difference. When I am rich enough you shall have the money, anyhow. I am sure you exaggerated your trouble. Tell the pretty Sita I shall send her a present for her wedding—and mind you get her married as soon as possible. Gopal is a good enough fellow, I am sure. Come, look livelier! and tell me that you trust me. I am still an Englishman, you know. Has the magic of that fact lost its charm?"

But the old man seemed petrified; and, feeling really uncomfortable now, the planter turned away, whistling.

"Obstinate!" he said, "always obstinate. Well, if you won't be comforted, you won't!"

IV

EXCITEMENT PREVAILED IN THE TOWN whence the Shastri had journeyed. The dreadful plague had already begun its ravages, and a wise Government was putting in practice stringent measures. Men stood discussing these at the meeting of the ways and on the steps of the temples. The inflammable young Indian had called monster meetings, and was airing his budding eloquence. There were Mahommedan meetings, and Hindu meetings, and meetings of both combined. In the great public library, in the heart of the city, had met the densest of these miscellaneous crowds.

Some greyheads had been on the platform, urging prayer as the best means of averting the disease; but they offered this suggestion cautiously, as if afraid of eventually attracting to their heads the blood of the community.

Up rose a young fanatic; the idea pleased him—he would urge it home. ('Twas Gopal of the Samachar.) "We will not go, my brethren," he said, "to the hospital. Our temples are our hospitals." (Loud cheers from the panic-stricken crowd.) "They will send carriages to take your sick away. Be not deceived: the carriage they send is—a hearse"—(groans)—"only you are made, my friends, to ride in it while the blood still flows in your veins, that you might chant your own death-song, and see, as in a vision, that which is shortly to be.

"You mothers! how will you feel when your dying children are snatched from your arms?

"You husbands! where is your manhood, that you can allow other men to hold the hand of your faithful wives?

"You wives! how will you abandon your husbands' corpses to contamination? ~> all exist only in family —> structuralism

"And, all ye fathers, mothers, husbands, wives, sisters, brothers,— ye who guard the religion of the nation, what of the caste rules broken? Ye Mahommedans, what of the spiritous liquors they will force upon you?" . . . (Here the storm which he had excited drowned his own vapourings; but after a while he was heard again.) "And not only when you are ill will you be taken captive, but when you are in health. Listen, fellow-citizens: this is the plan. First will come the sepoys—curse the renegades! every sister's son of them! They will come with their swords in their hands, and search our houses. The trembling woman and crying child will be brought into the fierce light of the open street. If you have but a headache, or a scratch on your small finger, you will be thrust into the awful hearse—the entreaties and cries of your relations and friends all unheeded. They, indeed, are driven like sheep, the dogs of sepoys biting at their legs, away from house and home, their little property being perforce abandoned to the greed of every passer-by.

"Near the Christian burying-ground is a row of white tents; there they will house them, safely out of the way, while they dig up your own poor dwelling, to look for treasure"—(hisses)—"while they unroof all the rooms, and burn all your property. That white canvas is the monument to a living grave, . . . for, when your friends return to you,— if they ever do,—what care have they for life, their loved ones gone, their fortunes to rebuild?

"And, look you, even white rupees will not now buy your ransom. While the sepoys were in command, the rascals, it was 'Off you go, Hari, unless you produce ten rupees.' But they say in the bazaar that the English soldiers will do the search now; the English soldier, and the doctor-memsahibs and sahibs. . . And though there won't be the oppression of the sepoy, you will certainly be carried away without mercy." . . . ∟ = indian soldier of British army

Thus the firebrand: and the poor ignorant people, panic-stricken, ready to believe anything, uncertain how to fight this unrelenting foe, listened to him, little wotting that they listened to their worst enemy.

CORNELIA SORABJI

Some of the leaders of the people did indeed try to get a hearing for wiser counsels.

"My children!" said one old Qazi. [*, Judge*] "Have you not come to me in all your troubles, public and private, these many years? This plague, remember, is God's visitation, not man's device. Are not the 'Government people' fighting it for themselves and their wives and children, as well as for us? And, indeed, more on our behalf than on theirs; for to infection our poor people are most susceptible. And do you not know that the doctor-sahibs go to the stricken with their own lives in their hands? Was it not but yesterday that one of the gentle English nurses took the disease and died? Day after day she had tended others. I saw her in the plague-sheds, always bright and cheerful, easing others' pain with such skill and tenderness. When she was ill herself and a special nurse was told off to care for her—'Send her to the wards,' she said, 'they need her, my own poor patients.'" (Here the women said "Hi! Hi!" in sympathy, but the young orator Gopal started ironical cheers.) "To-day two English doctor-sahibs are down. Some of our Indian doctors may take it too. Many are brave and fearless, their names are written in our hearts; but I ask you, my friends,—Why have certain of them themselves fled to the hills, leaving their charges? I ask you why the houses of some of our influential leaders are closed in the time of stress? Why are we left unshepherded?

"You are ignorant, my children. You do not know that if the authorities separate the sick from the well, the *evil* (in health) from the *good,* 'tis to give both a chance of life. Those white tents are no monuments to the expectant dead; they are indeed monuments, but to the care for us, of our rulers!

"Yon youth would remind you of plunder. 'Tis well. Ganesh the goldsmith was sitting at his door, covered with a sheet. I saw him; he was but a bit lazy, and a bit chill in the early dawn, . . . and he told me this, sanely enough.

"The policeman who walks the beat by his house came up. 'Ganesh,' he said, 'you are ill.'

"'You lie!' said Ganesh.

"'I will prove it,' said the policeman. '*Twenty rupees,* and a promise of twenty more in a week, Ganesh, or I will help you into the plague cart, which will be round presently!'

"Ganesh had no alternative, as you know. But, mark you, my children, 'twas your own brother who did that, not an Englishman. And 'twas his own evil act, commanded of no one. . . Our best plan"—

But this plain speaking did not suit the excited portion of the audience, though some others would have heard him gladly; the old man was easily overpowered, and thrust forth into the street. He walked slowly, with downcast head, pondering on life and death and human folly.

He was joined by an elderly Hindu, who had been giving him his support in the hall. "'Tis no use, Qazi sahib," he said; "would you counsel wild beasts or fretful children? And, mark you, though you and I know the foreigner too well to yield him aught but reverence, 'tis a *better understanding* reciprocally, which we want among the masses of the nations.

"Moreover, there is too much which is inevitable, which neither English nor Indian can help, at this stage. You know very well that 'tis not *death* which the people dread, but *contamination* and loss of caste. I, who am a Hindu, appreciate this more than you, notwithstanding your kind sympathy. See how wide a gulf lies between you and me in some matters! . . . And the best of intentions cannot meet some of our most perplexing difficulties at a time like this. The Government is conceding much, I grant. What will ignorance concede, when in this panic 'tis so hopeless to persuade it of even any need for concession?"

Thus talking they turned down a by-street into what seemed a *cut-de-sac*. A gateway standing yawning an invitation, and the passage through a small well-kept garden, brought them to the meeting-place of the Reformers, or more enlightened Hindus. The worshippers sat on little soft hassocks, cross-legged, on the floor, and the air seemed electric with devotion.

On a raised divan sat a yogi; there was a low table before him holding an illuminated copy of the *Vedas* and a few sticks of incense, which diffused a sickly sweetness in the close room. The man's lips moved in prayer. "*Om, Om,*" he said gutturally below his breath, while his body swayed to and fro. . . "Surely the 'cloven tongue' must now appear!"

He was clad in the pilgrim's garb, and his strong firm face betrayed many watchings and fastings. Then he spoke aloud.

"Let me adore the supremacy of that divine sun, the godhead who illumines all, from whom all proceeds, to which all must return, and which can alone irradiate not our visual organs merely, but our souls and our intellects." . . . It was but the translation of that mystic *Om*, which none may utter aloud and live, and which is the faithful Hindu's usual initiatory invocation.

For the rest of the prayer,—'twas only the sigh of impotence to omnipotence in this dread calamity;—the people listened with bowed head.

V

AND THE EVENING AND THE morning were the seventh day of the Shastri's absence.

"He ought to have been back three days ago," said Sita. "I should not have let him attempt the journey; it was selfish of me; yet he seemed so bright and hopeful."

"Mother!" wailed a querulous voice from a low bed, which had been carried into the sunlit courtyard to suit the child's whim, "Come, tell me pretty stories. When will grandad be back?' And the pretty story was so prettily told that the question about grandad was forgotten.

The child had been strangely languorous that morning, but this was nothing new in his usually poor state of health. Indeed, that he had any wishes at all was hopeful.

"Now tell me Surya!" he begged, and just as she finished—

"Lord of the lotus, father, friend and King,
Surya, thy power I sing!"

the rusty door creaked on its hinges and the old Shastri entered, led by a devotee, and looking terribly tottering and aged.

Site was at his side instantly, tenderness and anxiety commingling in her cry of welcome—and he was soon on a comfortable cushion, being crooned over, and revived with nice fresh milk and unlimited petting.

But he could not speak just then, and the faqir dare not; for, as Sita saw, he was a Maunee, and, as such, bound to perpetual silence. . . In course of time, however, she did hear of the luckless visit, but this much and no more, that it had failed; yet the marriage with Gopal was not pressed. The old man seemed too listless to urge anything.

Since plague regulations had been in force Sita had intermitted the daily visits to the god, and the terror of the city reached the little household but obliquely and vaguely.

The child still ailed: for the last day or so he had been feverish, and had complained of a bad head, and of demons who overmastered him in ill-matched wrestling contests—leaving him with pains in back and limbs. The child's head was full of strange fancies, born of the mythology with which his mother fed his baby cravings for a story.

Nor was he her only invalid; the old Shastri was comatose and inert, causing Sita much the greater anxiety of the two, lying dazed and quiet, and rousing himself only occasionally to query "What of the plague?" She nursed both with unfailing cheerfulness, distracting her father's attention as best she could, but keeping herself well-informed, nevertheless, through the old Mukti, who was sent on a nightly expedition of inquiry. One evening the woman came back horror-stricken.

"The search-party will be in our street to-morrow or next day," she said, "and the child and Shastri sahib will both be taken to the hospital for certain; and thou, Sita, wilt not be allowed to tend them."

No sleep did the darkness bring to the overburdened Sita. What was wisest to do?—wisest for them all: and should she tell the Shastri? The earlier part of the morning passed in alternate resolves and regrets, and finally she left Mukti in charge of her patients, and slipped away to the street then under inspection. She would see for herself what the dreaded visit might bode.

The silence of death seemed to reign everywhere. From the busy quarter leading to the temple the shopkeepers had fled. Barred doors sighed desolation. A few were chalked—"*Gone to Lanowli.*" One or two, more hopeful, added, "*Open again in a month,*" but for the most part the significance of the closed shutter was unrelieved. Now she turned into a street which was different: for the common country-made padlock was substituted a strong good lock and an official seal.

"They have examined this street already," she said, and she looked with interest at the dwelling-houses, and such others as showed signs of recent occupation.

On the doors were hieroglyphics which struck terror to her heart. Great red *noughts*—and in nine cases out of ten would appear a cross within the nought. . . "*Plague,*" it meant: "*death from plague.*" She needed no lexicon to expound that to her. The roofs, moreover, of such houses were untiled, the rough transverse beams giving every opportunity of in-draught to the still plague-laden breeze. Through an occasional chink in an ill-fitting door she could see that the floor was likewise manipulated, raked and uphewn.

Here and there a desperate thief, with hungry eyes and thin haggard face, was climbing down through the gap, in rash hope of possible treasure.

CORNELIA SORABJI

"Poor things!" said Sita, "poor everyone!"—and she was a-quiver with the apprehension of a like fate in store for her own much-loved home. But now there were indications of life. She had come upon the search-party. There were police sepoys standing at all exits and entrances, and a locksmith had just let into one of the larger houses a little party of soldiers and inspectors and a group of women, with a stray doctor-memsahib. In the middle of the road squatted coolies, beside light stretchers and ambulances, and in the distance was an unwieldy hospital cart.

Sita boldly joined the group at the door, and stood watching, unheeded. The house was evidently empty: the chief police sepoy was called in, and a thorough examination was made in his presence of every nook and corner. Here and there closets had to be broken into; all preservable goods were disinfected in the courtyard behind the house, while all suspicious rags, etc., were piled into a wholesome bonfire. Sita almost smiled at the little gods and goddesses sitting side by side waiting for a common phenyl bath.

Just as the party was about to issue forth, a box, cunningly placed under a side staircase, attracted the attention of the chief inspector. In it was found a poor old woman, in a dying condition. Air had been let in through a large hole made in that side of the box which was most remote from inspection, else she would most probably have been suffocated long since. She was trembling with fear, but tried to assure the searchers that she was quite well. If they *must* take her away, let it not be to the hospital. The lady doctor was very gentle, explaining that she would be well cared for and the Hindu nurse helped her on to the ambulance. "'Tis the deathbier, my son, my son!" shrieked the old woman, "and of what caste are they who carry me to my burning? My eyes are dim, I cannot see." There emerged from effectual hiding a shock-headed youth, seemingly half-witted, but so haggard and tottering that, at sight of the inevitable, he fainted dead away, and the two were carried gently to the nearest hospital.

A band of workmen stayed behind to untile the roof, and to dig up the floor, to do the usual lime-washing and sulphur-burning, and the party proceeded to the next door.

Sita sighed. "There will soon be *two* noughts on that door," she said; "on what door will they mark the crosses?"

She would peep at one more search, and then get back to her beloved charges. This was a washerman's house, and the man at the ironing-table sang out cheerfully enough, "Enter, enter, huzoor! no sick are there within these walls." But the gaiety was apparently forced; he whistled, and tried an occasional much-strained joke on the attendant sepoy.

A woman stood helping him, and her hand shook so that the irons rattled violently, and she had to busy herself elsewhere.

She was examined, but was found to be not otherwise than unduly frightened. One of the nurses now noticed a movement in the pile of white shirts and frilled blouses, which lay ready to be bound into bundles for delivery in cantonments. And she whispered the intelligence to the inspector.

There was a moment's silence in the gay whistle, but it went on boldly enough, till, the clothes being removed, disclosed an old man in an advanced state of plague. . . And so the sickening search continued: in some cases corpses were discovered lying among rafters; here and there a corpse would have been made even to simulate life. The great idea, however, seemed to be that cheerfulness disarmed suspicion; and the ghastly attempts at deception brought the tears to the eyes of the kindly nurses. . .

Sita had followed, fascinated, from one house to another, but now she turned and fled. "Were they coming to her? What should she do?"

But eleven o'clock struck, and the party was due at the subdivisional office to write reports. So Sita had a night in which to lay plans. Meantime the child had developed swollen glands; and the old nurse was in despair, because he could not swallow the glass of sweetened milk for which he was generally so impatient. The Shastri was just *tired*, every inch of him. "'Tis old age," he said, "*and* the planter sahib" (he added under his breath). But, hearing Sita's story, he roused himself. The party would most likely be at their house about eight o'clock next morning. He would climb into the leafiest of the trees—*wasn't* he a climber as a boy! Had not he ever told her? Ah! Sita should hear stories when they were all happy once more, in a dear little home, remote from this sickly town. Well, he would climb the tree, and the wee boy should lie quite still on his lap.

"You will be still, boy—won't you? *Such a game* of hide-and-seek, with the Sarkar to chase us!" And the old man chuckled, and the boy nodded, with bright, feverish eyes, eager for the fun. And then, Sita—what should she do? Sita should grind corn, and sing in the vestibule, overlooking the place of sanctuary and the lotus bed; so each would know what was happening to the other, and—did the party come again, once the inspection was over?

"No!" said Sita, "not if it were *safely* over!" . . .

"Ah, ha!" said he, "ah, ha! we shall eat our midday meal in peace. Sita, you shall make me little bhujyas of the edible leaf, you know, rolled tightly—how I love them, when *you* make them! And see, I did not tell you before, for I meant to return it, but, here—" and the old man pulled forward the inner end of his winding sheet, and untied something crisp, which had been knotted clumsily into a corner. "See! the commissioner sahib came to me, as I was coming away after that accursed visit, and he pressed this hundred-rupee note upon me. 'You will grant me this boon,' he said, 'that you keep it. My wife sends it to your small grandson, from her own little boy in England. You won't refuse it.' And there was the kind lady standing at the door of her tent, smiling and nodding; and while I hesitated she brought me the picture of two sweet little children—children like the baby Krishna sleeping in the cup of the full-blown lotus—and she made her husband tell me about them, and she said kind words in English. And so I took the money, meaning to return it later: but we will keep it now, Sita. The gods have sent it to take us safely away from here, so safely. Why did I not make use of it, these many days? My heart was full of hatred and bitterness, Sita, when it should have been full of gratitude. . . And I am punished."

"No, no, father!" she said; "'twill all be well yet, you will see." . . .

The little household was up betimes. Sita had got in some phenyl, and had flushed the drains, and had also had sulphur burnt in the empty rooms to give the search-party some confidence in her knowledge of preventive disinfection. She had determined that her visit of the previous day should be turned to every account. Her anxieties were all for her two charges. She was so well and strong herself; and a passing pain in her head was dismissed with impatience. And now the old man had been helped into the tree, and—yes! he was quite safe: neither Sita nor Mukti could discover stray toes or unruly wisps of hair. They covered his legs with a green saree, which harmonized cleverly with the foliage; and now, if only the boy would keep still! And, if only the old Shastri could stand the strain of holding him! "Was he comfortable?" asked Sita. "Yes! He would cling to the tree like death. Trust him!" . . . So Sita arranged herself in her pretty "lotus" saree, and sat to the grinding. It was a hand-mill; two circles of stone, one over the other, between which the grain was crushed. She worked it with a wooden handle affixed to the upper stone; but there was more singing than grinding, for the weight was over-heavy for the slender arm. The old Mukti was busy in the kitchen. . . And now, the door creaked. Sita waved and nodded reassuringly to the pair in the tree, and went forward gracefully to meet the searchers. Her veil was drawn with becoming modesty over her face, but she answered the inspector's questions herself, and in English.

Yes! the house was of course open to the usual search. Where would he begin? There were but she and that old woman on the verandah (for Mukti hearing noises had come to guard her loved mistress). Her husband was in England, and her father had gone a journey with the small boy, her son—(oh! may the gods forgive the gentle lie!). The head policeman knew her by repute and was nodding belief in the straightforward story, when the lady and nurses, who were somewhat in the rear, entered, and Sita sprang forward with a joyous cry. It was a new memsahib this morning, the doctor lady from her own mission school.

"Sita!" she said, "how glad I am to see you! and you are well, and alone? Yes, we must search the house, I fear. Ah! good child to be so careful! Everything smells so clean! Poor little Sita, alone! Where is the Shastri, and where my friend the baby?" So Sita had to repeat the lie: how she loathed it! Would it not be better to tell them all, and trust to their mercy? But they were in the verandah now, and examining the old woman.

"She's safe, Sita," called the doctor laughingly. And room after room was carefully searched, nothing being omitted, albeit appearances were so strongly in Sita's favour.

"We shall put a white mark on your door, Sita, to say we've examined and passed you, *for the present*," said the lady; "but don't be alarmed if an inspecting officer comes again shortly, to see that all continues well. And you are sensible—see, this is what must be done in case of infection." . . . Some terse directions followed, concluding with, "And you'd best take your usual exercise in your garden, it's safest so."

They were just about going, and Sita was already vowing offerings to every goddess of her acquaintance, when a dark-browed Maratha in the rear ventured a remark. "The lady has not herself been examined," he said, and he said it meaningly. "Moreover, she was yesterday in more than one house on whose door is now chalked the plague signal."

"It's true, Sita," said the lady. "You must be examined; I was forgetting. But were you indeed in stricken houses yesterday? Yet you disinfected yourself when you got home, surely?" Sita was compelled to confess that she had not; and, after the examination there was a brief consultation: then the lady spoke. "I am sorry, Sita," she said, "but I fear that I can't save you from it. The inspector sahib thinks you must go to the segregation camp. We'll make everything as comfortable for you as possible, and your old Mukti shall attend you. I myself, or one of the ladies whom you know best at the mission house, shall come and see you. "It will really matter nothing to you, this change, since you are alone."

"But," said Sita in dismay, "I promise faithfully to come to the hospital if I am ill. You know I have no ignorant prejudices."

"Ah, then, my child, be obedient now," was all the response she got. And even a farewell to the place of concealment was impossible. She daren't risk betraying them. But, just as the party was safely outside the door, she begged one indulgence.

"A last good-bye to my home," she urged, "in solitude. I shall be but one minute, by the lotus bed. Let me go alone, dear lady." And they let her, saving her the ignominy of a watch, though the Maratha wished it. Swiftly she sped to the tree. "Father!" she whispered, "keep a brave heart. There is food in the house: take it, and fly, outside the town, to Singhur. *Mind!* Singhur. You will be safe so, for at the railway stations they examine folk. Marothi, at the police station, will get you a palanquin. I will tell him as I pass now, and I shall watch for you by the segregation tents this evening at dusk. Your road lies past them, you know. I'll meet you at the old toll-house. I can run away; they won't watch me very closely. Good-bye, dear father. Good-bye, my son. The blessing of the great God be upon you."

But there was no answer, for the old man had half fainted when he saw Sita led away; yet so strong were both his will and that well-acquired habit to a praying Brahmin of maintaining any given position, that the clutch on the branches never relaxed its grasp, nor did the knees unbend.

"You were longer than a minute, Sita," said the lady reprovingly; but, as Sita's eyes were moist, she patted her hand and said no more.

VI

WHEN THE SHASTRI RECOVERED HIMSELF it was already noon, and though the sun blazed overhead he was stiff and cold; and—good God!—the boy lay dead on his lap!

It took him a minute or two to grasp the awful fact; but he had the spirit of another Eastern sage: *While the child was yet alive, I fasted and wept; but now that he is dead, wherefore should I weep?* Only, his sequel was otherwise. What mattered death?—that would come to all, sooner or later; 'twas contamination which did matter. So long as that was avoided there would be some chance of recognition in the re-birth. Yes, he must thank the gods for saving his boy from the hands of sweepers. . . He would take him himself to the burning ghat. So, descending with difficulty, he placed the boy on the green-sward. There was the suffering of a dumb creature in his eyes, but tears were a luxury denied to him; and so, indeed, was the indulgence of grief of any sort. Might not the party be back any moment! But when he strove to readjust the little burden he tottered and fell, and a nameless fear overwhelmed him. What if he should not reach the ghat? Down he was on his hands and knees, muttering to every god and goddess whose names his vast reading had ever suggested to him—praying for strength, a little strength. "Spare me yet a little while, O Vishnu! O Krishna! O Maroti! O all ye gods! And thou, O great Brahm, Source of Life, grant me but one short hour longer of the vital flame, . . . then quench it, if thou wilt, for ever!" . . .

He rose, dazed, and stumbled into the house, where, finding some still fresh milk, and the meal which they three were to have eaten in happy unity, he fed savagely: and, thus refreshed, returned to the cold burden. It was comparatively easy now to hoist it on to his back.

"No bier," he muttered; "they would suspect a death." So round his neck he clasped the little dead hands, and on his shoulder rested involuntarily the unresisting head, and from under the cloth with which he covered it there peeped one limp dead foot. . . Ah! the pathos of it!

The hour was auspicious. Plague officials were having a short compulsory rest, after the morning's exertions; heavy-eyed policemen dozed on their beat; and citizens, such as were abroad, were too occupied with their own ills to notice other folk. He had chosen the devious way through the garden wicket, and it was well, for the courtyard door was officially sealed.

Trudge, trudge, under the blazing sun, while the air seemed heavy with death, and a myriad thoughts flashed through the aching brain. "No fire," he said, "my child! no fire, no incense, no censer, no bier, no mourners; and thy father—God knows where! And *this* is the end of the house of Nagarkar, son of Krishnaram! Who can tell what will anger the gods, or this or that? And in what generation Nemesis will come?"

After a time his senses got dulled; the aged feet moved mechanically. . . Ah! there was the stretch of river coiling like a silver-scaled snake among the rushes, and there, on the farther side, was the strip of dry sand, the "mount of sacrifice."

The water was low, and the bund dry; he would walk across this, avoiding the weary bridge; and he would save thus, too, a good fifteen minutes. . . His feet held firmly to the sun-baked stone; but the water, as it splashed cool and joyous against the great boulders, touched something in his brain.

Was it last night he had dreamed of a bath in the river of life?

The river rose in the enchanting mountains of mystery, and it flowed through the valleys of time, and it made its way to the fathomless sea of eternity! And so kind it was to all who trusted themselves, unquestioning, to its swift current. Was this the river of life?

But here is the ghat; and the preparations are simple enough. A few dry twigs laid so, beneath and over the little dead "fuel." . . . "Do the sticks hurt, my child?"

A rope!—he'd never brought a rope! And he must grope about for some suitable flints for the initiatory spark. The search was slow; round black pebbles and yellow sand in abundance were there, but never a white gleaming crystal; and, O, God! dear God!—how the sun does blaze! And those brown-winged, strong-beaked kites, how they whirl closer and closer to the little upturned face! . . . But he had come now upon a mud-walled hut: he would beg a light and a rope, and perhaps a little incense.

"Peace be to this house!" he said, "peace! and the blessing of Vishnu! And may disease and death be slain—victims themselves, of health and life!"

But no one made answer; and pushing open the door he found a smouldering fire and a half-baked cake, and a woman lying on her back, lifeless, though not yet cold. . . "Death, death," he said wearily—"everywhere death!" but he took what he sought, and made his way back to the ghat.

The little corpse was bound firmly now, and the Shastri contemplated his work with some satisfaction. But—what was it that he had to tell the gods?—Something, something, *quick*—before the flame should reach the feet! Ah! he knew now.

"Great Brahm!" he said, "in this city of the dead no ceremonies have been possible. I have omitted the washings and anointings, the perfumes and the flowers; no gold, no gem has saluted the child's mouth, his nostrils, eyes or ears. I myself am unbathed. Forgive, great Brahm, forgive the omission, lay it not to his charge. . . *Forgive!*" . . . And now the flame was doing its work; the rope crumbled into ashes, the puny little body leapt into the air—and then—both hands were shielding the old man's ears against the sound of that awful combustion. . . the single salute as the soul entered the spirit world! . . .

He gathered his weary limbs together—yet, what need to hurry? Who was there who would expect him? Cruel time!—to claim the tender saplings and leave the old withered trunk! . . . Then a fierce impulse seized him—"The river of life"—ah! there was the reason of his solitude.

"Bear me gently, good river, to the shoreless sea of eternity!"

VII

IT WAS IN THE GREY dawn of the next morning that the segregation inspector, making his punctual way to his duties at the camp, found, on the road to Singhur, the dead body of a young and gently-nurtured woman.

Scouts and a litter were soon in requisition, and the official examination resulted in the verdict he had foreseen: death from that type of plague which lays a sudden grasp on the breaking heart. . .

And as night fell over the city, once more was an unresisting burden borne to the water's edge; while the watchman, proclaiming the hour, sang his usual lullaby—"Rest in peace, in peace, ye living! and, eke, ye dead! For love is stronger than death, than death, *than death!*"

LOVE AND LIFE

I

As thought elusive on a summer's day,
As full-choired music in the murmuring pine,
As rainbow'd beauty in the sunset ray,
As Love imprisoned in a heart like thine!

The women sate in the rose garden. It was at the zenana end of the palace, and bounded by high walls bristling with the spiky anger of the gaoler against all intruders. Not that walls of any kind were necessary; for those within would have died rather than creep outside their shelter: and those without?—Why, there were none, save serfs, who knew better their duty to their lord and the soil than to attempt to steal his roses, either through or over the wicket!

Well! but the women. There were two of them. Spring, and late Summer, in apparent age. Spring sat on a broad wooden swing, under a leafy mango tree. Garbed was she in silken raiment of tenderest green, wrought upon with some quaint workmanship of gold and silver. There was the elusive attractiveness of budding womanhood in her face and figure; and the sign unmistakable of budding love about the curve of sweet lip and droop of long-lashed eye. She sat contemplative, one little bare foot moving to and fro across the sward—sufficient pendulum.

Summer—a study in discontent and dyspepsia—had but just finished a game of cards with her serving-women, and was quarrelling on a point of social ethics, suggested thereby.

"Four queens to a king is the scriptural limit; 'tis much wiser to run to your full allowance, or revolt with a single favourite," said she. "You get them more companionable so. Now look at us. There sits the child, thinking her fool's thoughts, as if she were the wife of some peasant. She won't even quarrel as to whose jewels are the nicer! Of what use is she to me? Indoors her nose seeks her lesson-books; out of doors she is making garlands of her thoughts, to lay at, who knows, what dead shrine! Thinking to set the household a-wrangle for our diversion, I abused her waiting-women. But she smiled at me, and said she would gladly get rid of whichever I might name. Look at her, Moushi! What a child she is! And lovable too! Such a child might I have borne, an the gods so willed it!"

"Piari!" she called.

"Ay, Sandal Kuar," said the little swinger, tripping lightly to the group. "I was but just coming of mine own accord, to beg a story. Send these women away and let me rest my head against you, so. . . while you tell me of my mother. You knew her. Moushi says you did. And I want her to-day very, *very* much."

"Your mother, child? I never saw her, but I know of her, certainly. It is many years since she died, and you were such a child: 'tis impossible you should feel the mother-hunger. But I'll tell you. Know, then, that he whom we may not name, loved above all things the mother who bore him, and there was nothing he would have deemed beyond accomplishment had she but asked it. When we knew her she had renounced all earthly desires, and divided her time between entreaties for a grandson and thanksgivings for the single male who would so shortly light her funeral pyre. But on her son's 'name-day' she would lay aside the devotee, and come among us apparelled in garments befitting the queen she was. And she would tell us wondrous stories of her youth, of the lands she had seen, and the *darbar's* of the olden days; of kings who were gods, and women whose friendship was victorious over every accident. One such friend, she said, had been hers, and she still lived, but at so great a distance that nothing but a great joy or a great sorrow could now unite them. Well, just eighteen years ago—and yes! it's strange, this very day, we sate, the three wives of us, of whom I then was the last and youngest—we sate, those two who have died, I say, and I, in this same garden quarrelling or gossiping—who can tell which at this date?—but certainly bored with the monotony of life, and longing for diversion—when over that wall there—see!—beyond the white-starred jasmine bush, was thrown—a small ball! How we trembled! What enemy was working ruin to us? seeking to speak through closed doors! The two elder women looked at me. 'What means this?' said they, for once united in their anger. I, terrified, flew to the mother-in-law. 'Come,' said I, 'leave thy *puja*; balls thrown over the zenana wall, and a scratching, as with a sword upon the stone without. The gods defend us!' The old woman came at once, the prayer-wreath of marigolds still in her hand, and the mystic 'asking' look still in the faded eyes. She found the ball; it was a wood-apple scooped clean, and inside the red fruit-stripped cup lay a quaint-shaped amulet. The mystic look gave way

CORNELIA SORABJI

to one of eager surprise now, and she could scarce speak for agitation. 'Summon Ranjit!' she ordered (he was the zenana steward), 'and bid him pray my son to come to me without delay.' He came, straight from the council chamber; and we three covered our heads, and stood respectfully aside, though near enough to miss nothing. I jeered at the other two, behind my veil, and would have had them believe that it was my secret; but they knew better, and silenced me promptly. 'Son,' said the old woman, 'thou hast never denied me aught.' 'Thou knowest, my mother!' was his reply.

"'See!' she continued, 'this amulet—it belongs to the friend of my youth. On it we swore eternal friendship, and she promised me that if ever she were in need she would send me this. Her messenger should even now be without the gate. Tell me, my son, that which she might ask—hast thou granted it?'

"'Without doubt,' said the king, and the rusty little wicket in the gate yonder was forthwith opened, while Ranjit dragged in a travel-stained old woman, with a bundle in her arms! She walked straight to the mother, and did the salutation to queens—you know—the end of her cloth in her hand as she bent her forehead to the earth, once, twice, thrice; and then she went to the king, and at his feet did place confidingly her little bundle. *It* cried, and he laughed oddly, and lifted it off the ground—pulling aside the covering to disclose the sweetest little baby that gods ever sent to kings' palaces!

"We crowded round, forgetful of all etiquette, we four lone women; and the serving-women came too—talking, the host of us, with hand, and voice, and lifted eyebrow. Then the old mother seized the little thing and crooned over it, and—such petting as it got! 'Twas a marvel we rent it no in equal parts amongst us! *That* was *you*, child! The gods, great in mysterious working, had sent you to your mother late in life, beyond the time when women's bosoms are wont to heave with hope; and she, fearing the jealousy of her co-wives, had sent you straightway by stealth to this friend of her youth. These walls have heard your earliest prattle; and as the years marched forward, what was there to be done with you but the one thing? Of course it was irregular; no dower, no contract: but the king's mother wished it, and he loved you. *Phew!* as a *child*—'tis not the love women covet; but none of us know even that—so rest content."

The little Rani hid her eyes against her co-wife's shoulder. "I like that story, Sandal," she said. "And, what said you? He loved me '*as a child*.' I. . . like—that kind of love!"

The woman turned sharply to look at her; the voice thrilled even fleshless ribs! But the child had been quicker, and the tell-tale face was bent over her jasmine wreath-making, while she talked fast of other things.

"Oh, Sandal Kuar, I am getting so clever. I can read the Fourth Book in the vernacular, and—*He*—is so pleased. He is going to teach me English, and yes! also to keep accounts, and to read newspapers. And soon he says, I shall be quite as clever as the memsahibs, whom he sees in England, and sometimes here, and who talk to him as if—as if their brains were men's brains! Dost remember, the big state dinner, when the *Lāt* sahib came with all his retinue? I peeped at the gay banquet through the carelessly closed folding doors. It was wonderful! But I told him about it afterwards, and when I said I should never care to sit beside him at a meal, I far preferred waiting on him, he laughed, and pinched my cheek. 'And what of the game?' he asked. But I said, 'Oh, Presence, is that a thing to ask such as me? How could we ever run and beat balls with uplifted hand, in the sight of—the crown of our lives?' And he laughed again and said, 'I like you as you are, little one.' But I was so afraid that he would think I wanted not lessons either, and so I begged again about that; and he said, 'Yes! yes! have I not promised? You shall help me with my work, as did the wives of the kings of old!' Oh, shall I ever be clever enough, think you, Sandal?"

"Nonsense!" said her senior. "Life is only a play; we tire of first one toy and then another. Have I not wearied of my concertinas? 'Buy what you will,' said His Highness, and I bought near a hundred concertinas. How we played on them every hour, at first, my women and I! And now they lie broken and forgotten. So, you have bought books; they still amuse you. So the king has bought—*you!*"

"Oh no!" said the girl quickly. "He never bought me. Did you not but just now tell me how I came through the little-used wicket in the zenana garden?"

"What a child it is!" said the woman impatiently. "We are all toys, toys of time and space; some battered rather more than others, but all toys, and soon to give place to newer ones!"

But in her heart the child said, "No! no! *I* know. She cannot know. What is written is written. In the ears of a few does God whisper His secret. Shall they know who have never heard the whisper? Oh, *I know!* Thanks to the greatest of all gods, I KNOW!"

II

"There was the Door, to which I found no key;
There was the Veil, through which I could not see:
Some little talk awhile of Me *and* Thee
There was—and then no more of Thee *and* Me! "

"What art thou singing, Piari? Be quiet, child! He comes along the corridor." Piari hushed her voice, and made the customary obeisance with a pretty, shy bashfulness. "Come here, little one," said the king, after having greeted the elder lady with the honour due to her seniority. "What was it thou didst sing? It sounded to me like the murmur of the wind in the pine trees." "It was," she said eagerly, "it was the mystery of the wind in the pines, and of the sea when it moans, and of—and of—the human heart in pain"—And there she stopped, ashamed of her temerity. "I am sorry," she added; "it sounds not sense."

"Nor is it," said the elder lady. "My lord, these books are not good for her."

But the king laid a gentle hand on the bowed head, as she sat beside him in the place of her baby days. "What knowest thou of pain, child?" said he.

"Oh, nothing!" she assured him. "Thoughts come to me—whence, I know not. I hear things crying: the rose bush when I pluck a flower. 'Why did I bloom to die?' it asks. And my little bird, which dashed itself dead against the window-pane, keeps crying questions at me; and I could weep for having nought to answer. And in the storm I hear the sobs of the dying. . . and oh! I *hate* all pain. I *hate* the shadows. Why cannot the sun shine always, my lord?"

"It does," he answered gently, "for those who know you, little one. . . Now come! our books, for I have to leave early this afternoon. The minister comes with accounts, and crop-reports, and, I doubt not, an armful of petitions, to worry me." And in the mysteries of C A T with a C, and Rs and Ms for the creatures big and small that make sport for the purring favourite, she soon forgot all about veils and keyless doors!

Those tutoring times were the gladness of all the days to the much-harassed monarch. Sweet was it indeed to turn from the intrigues of courtiers and the battle with invisible foes to the women's apartments and that apt, eager little pupil. Sometimes they would sit in the rose garden, the pink petals falling on to her book and little bare toes;

oftener in the boudoir—the "Inglis-fassun room," as the senior Rani was wont to call it.

In course of time Piari knew enough to help with some of His Highness's vernacular correspondence, and was it not a proud moment when he praised her penmanship, and said she was of more use to him than many secretaries? The days seemed all too short for the things there were to read and learn. Newspapers and magazines were now littered about the "*Inglis*-room." And Piari would explain the pictures to the gaping women, and enliven the double retinue with news of the world without—of war and adventure. "How Lord Roberts' son won his V. C." was a favourite story, to be told again and again; and how his mother received the boy's decoration at the hand of "the greatest queen." They wept afresh and enjoyably each time. "And he was dead," they would say, "and never knew how he was honoured. But the mother, she knew; her heart would speak, even to his ashes."

The tale of the family of sons, all given to the Queen and the war, was also in frequent request.

"So should I do!" said the little lady proudly, and blushed; for, was there not—her secret? "Oh, good gods, make it a boy—*a boy!*"

The elder lady was very kind and unenvious in those days. "I saw you as a baby yourself," she would say; "I feel almost like a grandmother already." And all the women petted her, and made much of the usual ceremonies, and fussed about her health, and bade the priests say extra prayers. For as yet had there come no heir to the house of the kind Maharajah.

And Piari sat often, dreamily, thinking of her dear lord the king, and humming her pine-tree verse.

"There was the Door to which I found no key." *This* was it! The Door shut close, the Veil drawn tight. Would it be opened for her? *Would* it? Would the Veil be rent?

And one day, while the mystery was yet in the future, the king came in somewhat distraught. "Prepare," said he, "to receive another lady; she comes with attendants—some fourteen women. Give her my mother's rooms. The bride will be conducted to the palace to-morrow week at midday."

"As my lord wills," said the senior lady coldly. "We had heard nothing. It is a little hasty."

"It is, it is," admitted the king, "nor is it quite my wish: a political necessity." He looked not at the child, but said, for her special benefit,

"It is that Mussummat Kunti of whom I have spoken. She has been brought up somewhat on Western principles; has kept but casual purdah; is unbetrothed at eighteen; nor would any orthodox prince marry her. Her father and I had some political differences to adjust. I have been worried about them for some time; he suggested *this*, as a settlement. We were married at her father's state, on my last visit. . . What matters it? She will have her own rooms. Our happy afternoons will be as of old. Nay, she will be a companion to you, my child," he added, turning to her, "in the long hours when I must be away. And she will teach you far more than I can. She wanted to bring her English governess, but I have forbidden that, for the present. My mother was very orthodox; she would not have liked it. And now I must go; I have so many matters to arrange." And he strode away, clearly ruffled.

As the door closed behind him the women's tongues were loosened, and they spake many truths, yet mostly in innuendo, restrained by the pained, drawn face of "the child."

> *"Some little talk awhile of* Me *and* Thee
> Thee *was—and then no more of* Thee *and* Me*!"*

No more! *No more!* The lines beat themselves threadbare against the poor little brain. "She's clever. She knows more, he says, than even he himself. Can it be? And she will help him. He will not need me now. 'No more of *Thee and Me!*'" Was she pretty? "No!" said the serving-women. "We asked the king's men, who have but just come from her state. Fat and coarse-lipped—walks *so!* thud, *thud*, bandy-legged"— (mimicked the wit of the group).

"Don't fret, my heart's desire. She who bears the king a son is always favourite; none can displace her!"

"Is that so, Moushi?" she would ask wistfully. But in her heart, "Ah! a son, a son! Who knows if 'twill be so? I will test it. I will put two marigolds before the idol at bedtime, and if but one remains at to-morrow's earliest dawn 'twill mean a son!" The pendulum of her little heart kept a-swing 'twixt hope and fear over her childish experiments. Sometimes the gods would say one thing, sometimes another. "Oh, they mock me!" she would weep—"the Veil through which I cannot see!" . . . And, at last, the week was past, and—the music in the courtyard meant the coming of the bride!

Piari fled to her room and hid her face in the pillows, sobbing, *"No more of Thee and Me!"*

III

UNDOUBTEDLY THE FIRST AFTERNOON WAS the worst. The king was shy, and the women were frigid and silent; and—well! the simple question of manners made a difference. The new wife knew not apparently the etiquette of this zenana, and omitted the salutation so gracefully performed by her colleagues. She expected the king to greet her as the English Resident greeted his wife! True, she laughed good-humouredly, and tried a clumsy imitation, but the senior Rani was sadly shocked and prejudiced, and the serving-women were unanimously inimical.

"The child" was more concerned with her rival's personal appearance. "Oh, she *is* ugly!" she was saying in her heart, "and she squints, she *squints!*"

The days dragged wearily now. Three was a number difficult to manage. The new lady had ways and occupations in which the other two could hardly sympathize; and the king, seeing she was the loneliest of the trio, unconsciously got to talking English to her—discussing men and books, and the places she had seen; for she too had travelled.

And though the child understood, and though his caresses were still for her alone, she fretted her baby heart to pieces, whispering into the darkness every night, "No more, no more of Thee and Me!"

Day by day, too, the fancies grew. She would sit still for hours looking with unseeing eyes at nothing.

"The pine trees are calling" was all the answer she made to the senior Rani's motherly solicitations.

And one morning the good old creature violated all etiquette in her anxiety, bursting into the king's bedchamber with the enigmatical message: "The pine trees have called her!"

He slept, as was customary, under the drawn swords of his bodyguard; and *clink* went the steel in a noisy clash, at the unwonted interruption.

The king rubbed two fat fists into a pair of sleepy royal eyes.

"To *the inside*" (zenana apartments) "at once, Sandal Kuar!" said he sternly. "You forget yourself. I am coming!"

But, for all his bluster, a sad little voice kept sighing in his ear—

> *"There was the Door to which I found no key!*
> *There was the Veil through which I could not see:*

Some little talk awhile of Me *and* Thee
There was—and then no more of Thee *and* Me*!"*

No more! "The Door to which I found no key!" Had she found it now?

They searched all that bright day, in village and hedgerow, looking, with the stupidity of men, in all the most public and unlikely places. It was the senior Rani, after all, who found her. Unable to bear any longer the strain of inaction, of listening for footsteps which came not, she hastened to the rose garden, and out to the pine wood at the far end of the palace grounds. A tiny wail gave her her first clue: she ran to it trembling in every limb, at what it could not but mean. And there, lying in a very blaze of western glory, among the wild flowers, and on the sweet fragrant bed of the brown pine-needles, she found the child—and beside her, another.

"The pine trees called me, dear Sandal Kuar," she said, "and see! it *is* a boy! The gods heard me. Will my lord be pleased, think you? Oh, Sandal! I've found the key, and the Veil is. . . rent! But 'no more of Thee and Me; no more! *no more!*'"

The kindly Sandal Kuar was not long in summoning aid and getting the poor child home to the long-prepared welcome; but from the swoon into which she sank under the pine trees she never recovered. She had spoken truth. Rent was the Veil, but "no more of Thee and Me."

The "Pine-given" they called her little son. Since his coming no other has ruled in the palace near the pine grove.

I tell you, Stewart, it's playing the very deuce with a man's life to treat him as I've been treated."

"I thought that had been uncommonly well: by Fate certainly, in the way of fulfilled desires; and by your father, also undoubtedly, in the way of allowance. And what more can a man want?"

"Nothing—unless he's a married man."

"Ah! an indiscretion. You have my condolences, old chap: our follies always do vex us more than our sins, I know."

"Yes! and the offence is aggravated when you consider that it was someone else's folly. Listen, Stewart, and I'll tell you—I'm feeling communicative tonight, and this weed draws nicely."

The two men stood on the forward deck of the P. & O. s.s. *Khartoum*, bound for India, and now in harbour off Brindisi, awaiting the mails.

A bright moon looked down on the squalid town and the great expanse of sea, on the farther shore with its Turkish gardens and its tale of handsome brigands, and on the lithe Indian sailors, bending their supple bodies under the precious weight of the post-office consignments. One after another they crossed the bridge in well-trained rapidity. Pity the night was so brilliant! What thrill might not the darkness have lent to that scene of swift, noiseless activity!

Presently the foreigner spoke—"I was but seven years old," said he, "when my grandfather sent me to England, and, as you know, I have had no other home ever since. But there still linger with me Indian sights and sounds—music, and bright colours, and the scent of roses. I remember her, who must have been my mother, surrounded by chattering serving-women, who fed me with sweets, and flattered and spoilt me. But the memories all grow out of a noisy procession on a glaring day in midsummer. Dressed in garments of some startling hue, and smothered under the combined weight of heavy necklets and sickly odorous flowers, I rode gaily on a prancing nag, while the singers went before and the minstrels followed after. In the midst, however, was a single damsel, only—and she was not playing on a timbrel, but drumming two small henna-dyed hands on the horse's neck, as she sat astride in front of me. . . They tell me now that *that* meant my marriage! . . . It must, I think, have been almost immediately afterwards that I was packed away to the dear old dame's at Summerton, where we first met, you know, Stewart; for my memory comes to its *finis* about India when I have worried the past so far. And not a word, it's odd, has my father said on the subject all this long while; but in his last letter he tells me placidly, that both a welcome *and a wife* await me, in the land of my birth! I tell you, Stewart, it is infamous! She has most likely been kept a semi-prisoner all her life, knowing certainly nothing of the world, either as God or man has made it, and probably also nothing of books, even in her vernacular. I daresay she can cook a palatable Indian dinner, and scour the cooking-pans—but, well! it has not been fair to me at all. Systems cannot alter in a day, you will say. Exactly so! But why alter them at all in this one-sided way? Why create a false position for a pair of innocent children—Oh yes! I know it's hard on her too. Everything is a huge mistake: new patches can never mean aught but worsened rents to an old garment!"

"Poor old fellow!" said Stewart. "I never guessed such a complication. However, there'll be your work, you know, and perhaps she's not impossible, after all. You may even be able to educate her."

THE CONVERSATION WAS NOT RENEWED through the voyage, and, on landing, the young Indian doctor and his friend found that stress of plague-work claimed their immediate presence. The welcome and the wife had alike to wait. "Incidental freedom," said the Indian grimly; but indeed there was scant time for reflection, whether congratulatory or self-compassionate. He was on search duty, and hunting the dread infection from street to street demanded the exercise of every nerve and faculty. Ah, the sadness of it all! The feeble subterfuges, the brave fight against the most patent symptoms, the gasping attempt to propitiate the microbe—and finally, the sullen submission to Fate! The hearts of the two young doctors were heavy within them. Disease and death were sufficiently appalling—but with superstition for ally!—

Only this morning they had passed a mad procession carrying the dead plague-infected rats on spikes, while broken-hearted mothers and anxious wives wailed a propitiatory serenade, ghastly in its pathos! "We can't hold out any longer," said the Indian one morning after breakfast. "Write to headquarters, Stewart, and beg for a lady-doctor and a nurse. They must spare them to us. The poor women whom we find in the bazaar have to submit to our ministrations. What alternative is there? But the better classes, as you see, choose death rather than be looked upon by a man; and indeed I must confess that I greatly dislike having to search their houses. Don't you yourself agree with me, that it is our inability to deal with this class of patient which fosters the microbe?"

"Yes," said Stewart, "I do, and I'll write this very moment. The fear of the microbe is the mother of virtue."

"I wish it were the mother of sanitation," growled the Indian. "That's the kind of offspring I'm seeking just now."

In a week came the answer. The request was only just in time. An Indian lady with European qualifications was temporarily at the disposal of the chief medical officer. He had meant to send her elsewhere, but, as this was so sacred and orthodox a town, and as she knew the vernacular of the district, Stewart might have her for six months. They might expect her and a nurse in a fortnight.

"That's well done," said the Indian. "Now we'll get the thing under!"

She was tall and slender, intelligent and eager in face rather than pretty; and she carried herself with the ease and freedom of her race. Indeed her attraction lay in grace of movement, in fineness of proportion, and in a certain delicate sensitiveness, which could hardly escape even the least observant. For such work as fell to her she was pre-eminently suited—tactful, gentle, persuasive; and if she gave out so largely of her sympathising self to each sufferer, was that a fault? Her masculine colleagues thought that it was certainly so. "You'll break down," they said. "Besides, it's not professional!" And they devised common recreation to relieve the tension—golf, on the brown *maidan* to westward, clear of the temples and the odours; and tennis in the garden of the civil engineer, whose wife and the wife of the padre were indeed the only other ladies in the station, and both were ready to do everything that was hospitable and kindly. Such patches of sunlight were those afternoons!

Suffering and death and all ugliness were forgotten in congenial and healthful companionship. The girl had evidently been responsive to all the best influences of her Western training, while losing nothing of her own charming individuality. The effect was that of brilliant colouring under the brush of a master-painter. Even the women loved her. What of the men? Well! as to one of them, you must have guessed. That which happened was hopelessly inevitable. Could it be avoided between two young people of similar tastes, doing the same work, bearing the same sad burden, seeing the best and most unselfish side of each other, day after day, amid scenes which excited the keenest of sympathies? That it was a surprise to both, made the remedy no easier. The ludicrous side of it all was the similarity of experience. The obstacle was double-barrelled. There was a baby-husband as there had been a baby-wife!

"I always thought it very nice of him to allow me an English education," she said; "and I have often built him up round that one kind fact. But I begged a year's freedom on coming to India—and now, how ever am I to face that inevitable introduction? 'Where is he?' Ah! that I cannot tell; but I expect you would find him in his native village, a pampered only son, too orthodox to cross the waters himself, and managing the family property, in ignorant and comfortable self-satisfaction. What I cannot understand is my own liberty! There must be some third person acting a reformed up-to-date Providence, I'm sure! Till lately I've been so curious about it all, but now curiosity is swallowed up in loathing!"

"Pity we can't marry those two!" said the man.

It was the festival of the fire-god. "Though thou passest through the fire, thou shalt not be burned!" Who would make good the promise of the deity and face the ordeal? Through long months of prayer and fasting, certain rapt fanatics, and of good women not a few, had been preparing themselves to answer that question. And here was the very day at last! Down the heights into the hollows came the crowds of pilgrims—intending victims and applauding gallery all huddled together—one chattering, rattling, rumbling, seething mass, like to some mountain torrent seeking the level, and, when found, glittering light-imprisoned under the brilliant rays of a lingering sun.

By their dress shall ye know them—many-hued, many-fashioned— and also by their equipages. That long, low, wicker cart, likest to a racing-boat on lumbering wheels, has had other geographical genesis than that flat cradle-shaped construction of wooden poles and bambus. The great milk-white, soft-eyed bulls, easing tired necks with a graceful sweep of hoary tongue, have not before known as neighbour the small, perky, wiry cattle, tossing impertinent heads to the jingle of aggressive bells, and bellowing staccato inquiries.

But the crowd has one manner of encamping. Under each cart is tied a primitive hammock, and into this are thrown the squalling babies, safely out of the way, while their parents water the beasts and cook the evening meal. Secure are they here from intrusion. Do not the mountains stand sentinel? And are not the very clouds frowning a watchful "*cave*"? Yet it behoved them to do quickly that which they were purposing, for a wise Government approved not of the rash sacrifice of life; and even now some message of prohibition may be travelling from the camp of the nearest collector.

"In the blackest watch of the night—the inrush!" said the priestly herald, beating a muffled drum among the *al fresco* cooking-pots.

Gradually, like a long, stealthy shadow, silence creeps over the face of the valley, and out of the wordless darkness arises a great lurid fiery furnace. It shows the mass of onlookers, earnest, fanatic—ringing the sacred enclosure—a phalanx strong enough to withstand any band of venturesome intruders; and, at a sanctified distance, the knot of priests and white-robed devotees.

The head priest was speaking—"To the holy," said he, "this is no wanton sacrifice of life, but merely a hymn to the praise of the Deity—the rhythm of your bodies to the accompaniment of that angry roar. The *evil* do indeed take hurt, but is that not the just reward of their offences?"

"Let us go and see the festival," had said the doctor-girl to her friend. "My mother belonged to these hill-folk, and something stirs within me at thought of the great ordeal. I believe the instincts of the savage still survive. Do let us go, and I will—yes, I shall appear in the white garments of the devotee."

So they went, man and woman, in high spirits at the dubious adventure.

They arrived in time to hear the introductory address. The drums were growling now, and quaint pathetic incantations rose and fell on the midnight air. The first rush was just about to be made. One poor candidate has fainted. Carry her aside. Now!

They are through, unsinged, and a great shout of enthusiasm greets the semi-deities—canonization dearly bought!

But more stirring matters still are afoot. For now a group of young girls stand hand in hand, gladly responsive to the heavenly call, thrilling with the joy of martyrdom. But a moment, and the priest will give the signal for the fresh inrush!

"The gods will stay the plague," declares their messenger, "for the willing sacrifice of a band of virgins. Who will come, who will be the brides of death, to buy life for the millions? Who? Who? One short black moment for you, brave virgins. For others, years of glad happiness. See! the corn is ready to harvest, but the hand which would gather it is stiff; the grain is garnered, but the arm which would grind it is withered; the meal is prepared, but they who would eat it are dead! dead *and defiled!* with no sacred rites to buy them the best eternity. . . Buy you it for them, O virgins! *You!* Buy life now, and life hereafter—a double gift—and your own the hand to bestow it. Virgin life-givers!" . . .

In the silence one can almost hear life pulse! Then there is a sudden quick, convulsive sob—for, carried past all self-control, the doctor-girl has joined the band of vestal virgins. The word is given, and there they are, the white-robed seven, treading the flames.

"O Agni! do not burn them altogether," chanted the priests. "Let the eye go to the sun, and the breath to the wind! Go to sky or earth, as is right; or to the waters, if it is good to be there. But the immortal, the unborn part, warm it with thy heat and flame! Carry them in thy kindliest shape to the world of those who have done well!"

"*Peste!* Why sings he the death chant!" murmured the crowd. "It is ill luck!" And then—no one knew how it happened. . . "The doctor-lady!" they shrieked.

"She was tainted with infidel observances!" said the didactic priest; "the gods were angry!"

"She was not quick enough," said her companions. "Hi! hi!" mourned the multitude. Her friend alone said not a word. And she, poor girl, lay terribly scarred in the accident ward of her own hospital.

The end was not long in coming. "The decision of the gods," she murmured, and so slept, her hand in his.

POSTSCRIPTUM.—IT WAS A MONTH LATER, and the doctor sat in his consulting room. His face wore the look of the man to whom life has proved a resented discipline. There were arrears of correspondence clamouring for attention, and he settled wearily to the pile of multifarious envelopes.

Presently his eye flashed, and the sensitive mouth quivered, as he read a letter longer than the rest.

"Son," wrote, after much circumlocution, the father of whom he knew so little, "forgive the deception. It was part of your fate. The girl who worked in the hospital was your wife. We experimented for your good; but we were wrong. The gods resent experiments. In the path of orthodox monotony alone lieth safety. So perish all reform!"

But the man thought otherwise.

URMI

The Story of a Queen

Five P.M. and Saturday. Without, a cold wet mist, a grey sky, dirty streets; within, the curtains drawn, the cosiest of lounges, the softest of cushions, the fire crackling merrily, the kettle hissing gently—how nice it was to be warm, and sleepy! . . . Presto! They don't think long about things here. A moment ago that lovely red ball nestled confidingly between the peaks of those moss-covered mountains; now it has dropped, disappeared, gone to rest, leaving only its glorious curtains for us to look upon. Or, is this the entrance to the palace of some deity—into whose presence-chamber the sun has just been ushered? The strong mountains are on guard, and the stars in motion have played the royal anthem.

All here is in darkness, save for that reflection from the west. . . Softly—our way is through that wooded forest, under those great strong trees that embrace each other in their solitariness. Past the quiet lake, inside the gates. Another palace—large gardens, cool deep verandahs, marble halls, tall statues. Quick! Tarry not—through the courtyard. What is that? Only the sacred *tulsi* in its accustomed place. Grave men in red uniforms watch the buildings. Pass them by; they question not. At last! A low dark room—there, in that corner, on the bed. Hush! A moan—she is in pain—step gently. Poor thing! small and sad and beautiful! What eyes! What hair! What jewels! What lovely clinging saffron silk! Who hurt her? Her small hands are clenched—she beats her forehead—she calls on "Krishna." Now she rises—listen! She speaks.

"Bukku! Come near me. Are the women there? Send them away. I want you—only you. Listen, Bukku; there is not much time. What means this sickness? Is it death? Feel my hands; they burn. My head—it's like a hot stone, lying out in an April sun. I will not live the night. What say you?"

"Hush! Light of my eyes! My child—my flower, my tender lotus-bud! That will not be, that *must* not be. Your father is measuring the ground on a long pilgrimage to Benares. You will recover. Have you your amulet? Take hold of it; and see, here's a new charm. My grandmother learnt it of a faqir, and taught it me. It cured the good Akbar once, when he lay dying. The little Gulam went up to the hills

CORNELIA SORABJI

this morning, and brought me the healing herb from a far-distant spot. See, too, my bracelets—they are with the priests; they will appease the gods. They were good gold. Nay! my beautiful, you will live many years. My treasure! My precious stone, the worst is past."

"No! Bukku, you are kind, you love me. You are the only true creature I have beside me. All else are false, and mean me ill. They are like the hooded cobra, they sting me in the grass. O Bukku! I have not loved this royal state. And they love me not here. Would that I were home again, on the cool soft banks of my own river. Remember you, Bukku, how the lotus floated on the water, and the plantain trees spread their green shade over our heads? And my father—my dear kind father—how I read with him, seated on his knee, stories of early times when the world was young; and of the beautiful Sakuntalla, and the poor Nar Jehan; and those verses of Kalidas, when he read them to me—'twas like the little summer brook playing with the pebbles— so pleasing to my ear. . . It's all over now. He will miss me, my poor old father. And perhaps he, my lord, whom I may not name, *perhaps* he will sigh for me, and say 'She was young, and the gods made her beautiful, and—she is dead.' And he will be just a little grieved, and bid them play sad music, and feed poor Brahmins in my name. . . Then, he will go out and hunt or shoot, or sit with his councillors and forget me quite. I've loved him, Bukku. He was good to me, and strong and wise and kind; and when I talked to him of my early days and pastimes, and the things which I loved, he smiled and said—'It is not so with all my other wives; they know not what to talk about; they have not read your favourite books; they cannot read; they care not what transpires in other lands; they ask me for new jewels and prettier clothes; and look modest, and sometimes beautiful; and that is all; but you.' . . . And once he praised my wisdom, and said he would I shared his throne with him. See! keep you this letter; when they lift me on the bier, and bear me to the burning ground; and put the torch to these cold limbs, go to him, put *that* in his hand. It's not long; just one line—he will know and understand. . .

"And now, Bukku, quick! the child! My strength is failing. Bring him to me—nearer—lift him up. How beautiful he is! His eyes, how large! how dark! how deep! I feel I am looking into a well of light, of sunshine, of clear cool water. His small round arms, how soft they are! He smiles! poor child: he wants me—and I go, whence I return not, unless per chance as some small reptile, or a tree, or a flower.

"I would it were a flower, and that I grew where *he* would touch me, and feel my petals, and say 'I like that flower, it is as pure and fragile as my little Urmi.' . . . But, when I'm gone, take the child, carry it hence. They mean it harm. You have nursed me—nurse it: but *hide it*—hide it safely from them—from Afzul. My father will pay you, and will see to its future. Now, while it is young and helpless, you must love it and care for it. Tell it of me and of its father. . . but let *them* here think that it is dead. You know what to do; some poor baby you will purchase in the market, will have a prince's end. . . I will tell you all, Bukku—you shall tell my father. Tell him how they hated me here. You remember, when I came, how they looked at me and shook their heads, and said a 'God forbid' because I read and wrote? And when the king, our lord, favoured me above them all, and sought my presence, and listened to my words, I heard them whisper. 'Bold minx!' they said, 'child of the Evil One! She knows what it does not beseem women to know, for she reads and writes as if she were some common clerk. And when she talks to *him*, she lifts her eyes and looks upon his face. How know we that in her distant home she did not break her *purdah*? We hear her father taught her many things which he learnt of the Feringhee.' . . .

"And my women who loved me, they turned against me. All but you, Bukku, whom they did not dare to touch; but they kept you from me, knowing you loved me. I was wretched, and wrote my father word that they all looked coldly on me. He said, 'Try gifts, try gold and jewels.' They took them—but it made no change; and I would I'd never left him—but for the king whom I loved—yet him I seldom saw. After the boy came, things were worse. Lying ill here one day behind this heavy curtain, I heard them talk, and Afzul was with them, and he said 'Would that the king had hearkened to my words, and taken to wife the bride whom I had chosen. With this one, I have had no commission; and she is the child of the Evil One. See how she has bewitched the king. He praises her looks, and her learning, and her ways, and now there is an heir, his regard for her has grown tenfold. We must *remove* her and the boy. Say the word: it shall be done!' And then, Bukku, *his* mother, whom I had tried to love as my own, said 'You know your work: *do it*. I give you leave: she has come between my son and me!' And Afzul—how he looked! I saw his eye gleam and he swore an oath by his father's head. He is a terrible man. Shield my boy from him, let him not see his face. It would haunt his baby days—it would make a stain on his mind. Oh! would I were here to protect him! But what power would I have? It would but make matters worse, could I intervene. *You will care for him, Bukku—you and my father. The king—he cannot: he must think him dead.*

"You see *that* . . . Afzul. . . did. . . his work. . .

"What is this, Bukku? Is it—*death*?

"My eyes grow dim. Call on Krishna. I am falling—hold my hand. . . The lord, my king—would he were here! . . . My love! I have loved you much: love me a little."

. . . Through the open door streamed in the moonlight and kissed the lovely figure as it lay; from the hills came the weird bark of the jackals; an owl shrieked in the mango grove. . . What is that? the deathwail? They know, then, that all is over. Is it well with them in the agent's sanctum? in the zenana? in the servants' courtyard? in the king's chamber? Is it well?

Seven P.M.—The fire is low; I am cold. Was it only a dream? Alas! would it were! It was the wail of some poor child in a London street. And it wakened the memory of other sad things in far-distant climes, across the seas. . . Poor Urmi!

GREATER LOVE

I t was the month of May, and Kamala-bai had a *kunkun* party. They all have *kunkun* parties, the newly married, when "the year's at the spring."

"For five years," say the sages, "worship Ana-Purna, the Deity of fruitfulness."

Little Kamala was quite accustomed to the dissipation, this third spring of her married life; but it had lost none of its excitement. She was up betimes, watering the little patch of grain near the tulsi tree ("let no good wife omit to sow and tend the golden grain!"), cooking the sweet confections, and plastering afresh the bare mud floor. Then there were the decorations in white chalk—big fishes for good luck, and all the impedimenta of her own particular patron saint. How clean and festive it looked, to be sure! And Ana-Purna herself had a new coat of red paint, and sat smiling in her niche, while at her feet burnt the cotton wick that acts taper to the cocoanut shell of the East.

("We are offering thee the best of our melted butter to-day, O Ana-Purna! Doth it not please thee?")

The altar was a three-tiered erection of packing-cases, covered with an old piece of *kincab*, and the assortment of gifts was eloquent and picturesque. The fruit of the earth—bright red pomegranate seeds bursting through their thick brown hide, small yellow bananas, the purple and green grape, the striped watermelon; and the fruit of Kamala's morning labours—round creamy *laddus* and neatly rolled *puris*.

"My thoughts too should be on the altar," had reflected the maiden. And so you found on the lowest step, as if in apology for the innovation, some well-thumbed lesson-books, and the gayest of her baby's garments—a cloak with peaked cap and tassels, ornamented with bright tinsel.

For the rest, the room was absolutely bare. Kamala, dressed in a red silk saree and with her hair well oiled and braided, stood at the door near the outer quadrangle, but well hidden from the road by a great gateway.

"Welcome! O mother of a man-child!" said she as she pressed between two palms the hand of the first comer. "Your foot is auspicious. The gods do so to all my guests!"

Individual greeting was accorded to each, after her kind (Kamala was a born hostess), and then she turned to her symbolic duties.

Beside the altar were placed wicker baskets of golden grain, the wheat gleaming in the sunlight. Kamala seized one of these and carried it round to her guests, each woman opening the fold of her draperies, while Kamala poured in a generous dole.

"The earth has yielded us of its best. May you do likewise for your country and nation, by the blessing of the Lord of Creation; O mother, I pray for you!" was the meaning of her action. "And for *you*!" "And for You!" to the ladies in turn, till basket after basket was emptied.

The women were talking loudly and fast now, commenting on the decorations and the refreshments and on Kamala's ingenious altar.

"'They get some notions by going to school, these children," said one sourvisaged old dame. "You can't call the books and clothes orthodox; the practice is undoubtedly new, and therefore to be discouraged. Time enough they married her to that lout of a Vakil. He feeds well, and keeps her busy over household duties. I warrant she wastes money, though. At what rate did you buy those grapes, Kamala-bai?" she called.

But Kamala was at the other end of the room, emptying her last basket.

"O Matha Shri!" she was saying to a gentle-faced matron. "I pray most of all for you. See! You shall have this entire basket of wheat. Perhaps Ana-Purna will incline her ear, and give you the desire of your life. And listen, I pray a new prayer for you. 'My prayers are *yours*, but only in order that the gods may reward *me*,' is, as you know, the usual form; so that all this feast but means my cry to God for mine own self. And in truth it is, so far as all those women are concerned. But when I come to you I say, 'I pray for you! May the gods hear me, and give you (not me) a son!' Do you understand, Matha Shri?" she added wistfully. "I mean it, truly: even if the gods are too busy to give both of us—that which we desire. And I've said the same prayer for you at every *kunkun* party this year. It will come right, you'll see!" And she looked down into the old wrinkled face, radiant with love, and with a new something to which Kamala could give no name.

"*Are*, Kamala! art deaf?" was shouting Chimini the shrew, across the room. "'Tis ill luck to talk so long with Matha Shri, wife of the pundit. You ought to forbid her your *kunkun* parties: have not the gods cursed her in that no son is born to her house? And she is half-witted: any other woman would have *managed* things, or brought to her husband some pretty, young bride as co-wife; but she bewitches him, so that he dare not marry another!"

The keen old face quivered with sensitiveness as the cruel words reached her in her corner; and Kamala put a protecting hand on her shoulder.

"Matha Shri is a guest whom I would never spare," said she; "to me her very presence means blessing."

But Matha Shri had risen—"Your favour is pleasing to me, my child. It makes gladness in a heart that is often sad. Yet the woman speaketh truth." She looked round slowly at one comfortable matron after another. "This gathering of—*those-who-have-attained* and—*I*? No! it certainly is not beseeming that you should anoint my forehead in their presence. *And yet*—I wanted—the sacred red *kunkun* at your hands, my child. . . But even a single luckless wife breaks the current, they say. No! *No!* I must go. . . Who knows for what sin of an earlier birth I suffer now? This alone is certain, the gods are just. Peace be upon you! . . . My lap is full of the life-sustaining grain, each 'bead' a prayer!"

And before Kamala could prevent her she was at the wicket. "A good thing, too!" declaimed the shrew. "It is never wise to tempt the gods too far. Why do they put these unmistakable labels of ill luck upon such people, but that we may know whom to avoid, especially upon our feast-days?"

"Yes! yes! so it is. Wisdom cometh from her mouth," said another. "You have a kind heart, Kamala, but beware where it leads you. We cannot separate ourselves from our actions, and if you touch a luckless thing—*Toba!*" (God forbid!).

"*Toba! Toba!*" echoed all the women, beating the palms of their hands upon their cheeks.

Kamala was silent, as became a well-mannered Hindu maiden in the presence of her seniors. But there was a viciousness in the jerk with which she anointed each virtuous forehead. "Daub, daub," she went, with the slimy red stuff out of the silver pot, till each guest bore her stigma of wifehood at the hands of her hostess.

A *kunkun* party is a good old custom, and picturesque withal.

And now they had all gone; garlands of flowers and gifts of fruit were Kamala's material good-bye; and indeed the departing guests looked like peripatetic harvest festivals. For no one ate on the premises—oh no! Eating and best clothes were incompatible.

But Kamala sat thinking of poor Matha Shri. "She shall have a large dole of fruit and comfits, anyway," she said; and one of the wheaten baskets was filled to overflowing, and thrust into the storeroom to await convenient transport.

Meantime the luckless lady had avoided the crush of the thoroughfares, and lost herself in such a labyrinth of byways that she was now in a grove of mango trees overlooking a lake and its island temple, many furlongs distant from her home. "'Tis well," she said, looking around her with a bewildered air. "The thoughts crowd my mind like spectators the exit door of a theatre I must put them in order. Nano is a good man. The gods have blessed me indeed. How little that jeering one knew the truth. 'Marry another woman, my lord.' (Ah! have I not said that too? But it must be said again.) 'Marry another—a widow if you will: or—my cousin's pretty daughter—the child we have brought up as our own.' You've watched her often, I've noticed, as she flitted about the house—such a buxom maiden, soft-eyed and winsome withal. And you have been loth to part with her, even in betrothal. . . Could it be, that, for all your refusings and dislike of multiple wifehood, you had some hidden wish. . . some day. . . *Could* it be! Ah! Nano! I begged you to do it—though not thus definitely, with a name, a face to the request. Perhaps it would be different if I could do that. . . Oh, gods! it's hard when it comes as near as this to—to arranging for one's own supplanter. . . And yet, that love is poor which yields not all. 'And thine own self beside,' . . . *of course* if it would help him. 'A son to light my funeral pyre, to pray for my soul!' . . . Yes! he murmurs that even in his sleep, and knows not how he wounds me. He shall have one, cost what it may. . .

"'She should have managed it,' said the old hag—'half-witted creature!' 'Managed!' . . . Ha! I know. The feigned seclusion, the purchased fondling—a faithful nurse! No! *no!* No deceiver is the luckless Matha Shri, despite her barrenness."

But the tempter persevered, and she hid her agonised face on her bended knees, and stopped her ears to get beyond his voice.

Hundreds of women did it: Nano would not know: Nano loved her. . . Well! call it adoption. Was not adoption a religious duty? Why, it might even be Sahai's son—Sahai married safely to that young accountant from the "Company" bank. Sahai would keep her secret, and Nano would be pleased—and she herself? Why, she might sit in the company of the successful, and speak to her enemies within the gate, secure from all reproach. The little son, too, how she would love him. How she would help him buy back the lost opportunities of those sonless years. . . Yes! surely it was the right thing to do. Why, her arms could almost feel his little confiding weight already. . . If it might only have been her very own: the gift fresh from God's great hand to herself—not a gift snatched from another. If *only!* . . . but that was clearly withheld. The gods would not treat with her for any sum. And such bargains she had offered them!

Ah! well! the incidental child it must be, with Nano as chief-deceived. . . "It's for *his* sake I do it," she said, raising a determined hand preparatory to the vow of approaching motherhood. "I've offered him another wife, he will have none of her. What remains but that I should sin? . . . And what said the Shastri from the north? 'Sin without detection, is sin absolved.' *Is* it?" . . .

Tinkle, tinkle, said the temple bell. It was the sunset hour, and the blind old priest was sprinkling his sacred bull with holy water and marigolds and unintelligible mutterings.

Tinkle! Tinkle! Matha Shri sprang back as if from an assailant. She couldn't; that familiar sound brought back the years, the long years of devotion and rectitude. "Thy right is to action, not to the result!" said the Bhagwat Gita. Yes! to *right action* . . . No! *No!* Prince of Darkness, Love *shall* conquer! . . . And did she realise what it meant to relinquish for ever the chance of motherhood. . . Did she? . . . So she wrestled with herself, the tired waves of thought dashing themselves in vain against the resolution which she knew was, after all, her rock of salvation—till, at last, the smile of Heaven lay on the darkened words as she sought her homeward way.

"All is living that was dead," she said. "The thought born of this hour must be my only progeny. Will it buy me the right of entrance into heaven? God knows! And He knows, too, that I would relinquish even that chance, if it would buy my Nano his living, pulsing son!"

"So late! Matha Shri!" said Nano when she entered the courtyard. "Why! but for the pretty Sahai yonder I'd have starved. She hath a very dainty way of rolling the leaf bhujya. I would have you learn it: and the very way she offers me the post-sacrificial basin is a poem. . . Ah! that accountant will be lucky—if he gets his way. I've been thinking on that matter lying here in the quadrangle. . . Look at the child now, scouring the pans: saw you ever such turn of wrist?

"But where have you been?" he queried sharply.

"Only to Kamala's *kunkun* party," said Matha Shri, "and then, on my way home, I—lingered—in the wood—by the island temple—thinking."

He noted her confusion, and his face hardened. "Kamala's *kunkun* party, with no mark on your forehead! And, the island temple *on your way home!* Lie not to me, Matha Shri. I know the town; the island lieth two miles out of your road to and from Kamala's. And I know, too, how women should return from *kunkun* parties. If you bear not your red label show me at least your gifts of fruit and grain."

But poor Matha Shri's arms were bare. For, indeed, she had forgotten her wheaten store in the forest.

"My lord!" she stammered, "I do not lie—the wheat is bound safely within my best yellow shawl, and lieth under the trees but now. If you believe me not, ask Kamala about the *kunkun* party. . . You never doubted me before, my lord!" she added sadly.

"Enough!" said Nano. "Excuses at your seared age are unseemly. Heaven knows you need the prayers of happy mothers! I would have forgiven you had you confessed to lingering at Kamala's party. But I begin to doubt that you ever went there at all. . . Ah! Sahai child," said he, brightening, "opportunely arrived! Bring me a new packet of beetle-nut: the one thou broughtest me but now was a veritable snare for the appetite—just the right admixture. And I like the little kernel of black tobacco which I did find in its inmost heart."

Matha Shri watched and listened. "The gods do sometimes point the way," she thought. And then, to help the best part of her nature, she turned to Sahai with a smile and a kindly pat of approval. "Run along and make it, child!" she said.

They were alone now, those two middle-aged folk. Matha Shri sprang to his side. "Life of me!" she said impulsively. "I've often bid thee wed another; and, crown of my days, thou hast refused. But it was my fault. I should have urged thee: the years fly past. I should have brought some young thing to thee, leading her by the hand. I should have prepared the marriage portion. I should have summoned the priests. Mine has been the error in accepting thy sacrifice. But see! I will have it no longer. Marry our little Sahai. Comely is she in mind and body! And the dower which her father left her will buy thee the adjoining field for that scheme of thine touching the zenana hospital, and thus maybe win thee thy Rao Bahadurship from the new *Lāt* sahib. Do it, my heart's blood. I wish it. So happy I should be in thy happiness! The years of personal joy which have been given me are more than fall to the lot of the barren. . . I have my memories. . . My lord! this thing is required of thee."

But Nano, because the thing was in his heart to do, said crossly, "What fool's talk is this? It would almost seem as if—thou hadst—a motive! Go!" (and he pushed her roughly away), "go, and eat the food which thou didst neglect to cook!"

A week of days followed—Sahai grew in favour with Nano, and Matha Shri was restless. . . She would wander to the island temple, when the day's work was done, for she felt that some thought would come to her here, some thought of God to help her husband. At last!—she knew it—in a flash. Nano did not like to go back upon his word. In the council of the reformed, around the village tree, "I wed but one wife," had he said. And now, if he wedded Sahai, they would jeer at him: his opinion would lose weight among the elders. And yet—Nano would like—to wed Sahai. . . Yes! she saw that! And he would like to wed her for more than scriptural reasons. Ah! . . . if there were no Matha Shri all would be well. . . *What had she said?* If there were no Matha Shri. . . why, there *should* be none!

She went home, almost gaily. "My life!" she said, "I have made a vow to feed the old faqir who lives on the top of the mountain pass—thou knowest: and to-morrow my vow will crave redemption. Sahai will take care of thee: I will shoulder my gourd of oil and the offering of ground-nut cakes, which the god loveth above all things, as thou knowest; and ere cock-crow I shall be on the mountain-side."

"But the passes," said Nano, "are not safe. There have been landslips with the heavy rains."

"What matter?" retorted Matha Shri—"gods cannot be defied, least of all by the barren. *Farewell!* Never was childless woman so happy as hath been thy Matha Shri!"

It is three years now since the journey to the mountains. The god digested his ground-nut cakes; and over the pass went Matha Shri to a cave of which she had heard in childhood. Untenanted it had been since the death of the last *gosain*, many moons gone by; and the idol in the niche looked neglected and surly.

Roots and berries, and water from the mountain stream, and in the time of dust-storms, bright red locusts, made diet fit for princes. And night and day she blessed her love, who dwelt in the village under the mountains. . .

Sometimes the pilgrims would linger and gossip. "We must hasten ere night overtake us," they would say—"for, but so many years ago, a poor woman from the village yonder got lost on the far side of this pass."

"*Did* she?" would ask Matha Shri.

"Ah! but yes! you villagers never come over the pass, or you must have heard the story. She was the wife of Nano the pundit, a good man and true. And strange it is, but it was in her very loss that he was blessed: for she was childless, and Nano (who had, you must know, some queer notion about but one wife at a time!), thus released, married her cousin—a buxom lass. And now, behold, a sturdy son runneth about the courtyard, and joineth the village councils under the pipal tree. Shouldst see Nano, holy mother! No prouder man in this generation, I'll warrant. . . And time, too, say I. . . the years were striding on."

"And what say they of—her? Is there no talk of—her who was lost?"

"No! none! Except—that people wonder at the great love which Nano bestowed upon her, in refraining from using, through the long empty years, his privilege as a sonless Hindu. That was her only glory, this love of Nano's. And her name shines in the glow of it, as the western sky when the sun is in the east. Yes! Nano sought her on the mountains, and even grieved for her awhile; but when she came not, why, there was Sahai so handy. And they even say the old wife wished it. Chimini, the village shrew, suggested things sinister about the visits to the island temple: but no one heeds Chimini."

Nor did the devotee. . . "So," she said in contemplation, "Nano's great love for her is her sole right to remembrance. . . You have laid hold on a great truth, oh pilgrim. May the gods bless you with the blessing reserved for the truth-finder! Peace be with you!"

"And with you dwell peace!" came the voice of the pilgrim through the gathering shadows.

Behind the Purdah

I

A STRAGGLING BUILDING WITH A spiked gateway, sadly out of repair, and needing manipulation in the opening, as it led through a bare courtyard to a portico that did its best to be imposing,—such was your introduction to the royalty of Balsingh Rai, of an Indian principality. And if indeed the iron and mortar had failed to impress you, there was always the chance that the ill-dressed, ill-drilled guard would excite what was lacking in sentiment.

But there was time for a regular series of impressions to lounge through your unoccupied mind. The opium-eating courtiers around his magnificent Highness believed in admitting you to the presence in—detachments. The more abject you felt, the more likely was it that you would appreciate their pinchbeck glories; and you sat on, in the *darbar* vehicle, the two lean horses foaming with the drive from the guest-house, under the weight of a not too modern chariot and a harness patched up with strips of soiled rag or old packing-cord.

Along the unwashed stone verandahs were disposed *darzis* (tailors) of varying capacity. Their overseer sat holding some cheap Manchester print between the toes of his right foot, the while he clicked the unerring steel of the workman whose craft had come to him, like his existence, from his immediate antecedents. Curious garments they were which he cut—loose, shapeless coats with tight interminable sleeves; and he threw them now to this, now to that subordinate, who whipped a long piece of cotton off a small white ball, and requisitioned both toes and fingers while he helped the creation of the coats through the next stage—in preparation for the large important man at the sewing-machine. Yes! a veritable sewing-machine it was, and the colony and the state were rightly proud of it.

Before you look further, you should note the way the men work. 'Tis non-Western, topsy-turvy, the needle pulled away from you, and travelling therefore, from left to right of the seam, instead of *vice versa*. In a group by themselves sit the gold and silver embroiderers—lean men with keen faces and bent backs. They sit on the floor cross-legged, and the most beautiful designs grow under circumstances and with the aid of implements primitive in simplicity. Beside each worker lies the bullion (gold and silver in tiny spangles or delicate wire lengths) in some rough receptacle—an old newspaper, perhaps, or the contents of your waste-paper basket. The design is chalked out on the velvet or satin; and he sews the bullion on to this, running the sharpest of needles through the wire, which he has first snipped to the size required. The manipulation of that mass of glittering gold and silver becomes fascinating,—But here is Chunelal the herald. Miss Rebecca Yeastman, the lady-doctor, through whose sun-spectacles we have been looking, is summoned to the *darbar*-room.

Tall is Miss Rebecca, and spare, and angular. As she alights, her *chatelaine* jingles ominously. Have you ever noticed how much personality there is in a jingle? There is the cheerful jingle of the maiden of seventeen—an inviting tintinnabulation, saying, "I am coming, play with me, laugh with me, waste as many precious minutes as you dare!" There is the decided resonant clash of the elderly matron: "I have come," it says, "to set things straight;"—don't you hear the sound? Then, lastly, there is the mean between the two—the confident, active jingle of the woman of business, not enticing, but yet not jarring, just pleasantly negative. "I know not what your work may be, but I've come to do mine, and to do it well;" and at the sound all idlers despise themselves, and slink into unseen corners.

In India there is a further jingle, the jingle of the domestic—"rings on her fingers, bells on her toes;" but her ditty is, "This is my bank! my bank! In this showy, noisy form I carry my savings."

Rebecca Yeastman was of the third category, and the tailors did instinctively sit the more upright as she passed them, while sleepy Hari in the corner rubbed his eyes, and cracked his toes, and fell vigorously to his tacking.

Not a whit bashful was she, as she followed her guide up the marble staircase; the outlook was improving, but her environment very seldom affects a woman of Rebecca's calibre. For so self-possessed, brisk a person, her walk was a surprise; 'twas rather like a camel's,—head protruding, steps long and halting—but it did, nevertheless, suggest dogged steadfastness of purpose; and she was a thoroughly good creature, every faculty of her, of that you might be certain.

"Lady sahib will wait here," said the man. "Ranee sahib have not yet had permission to receive. Rajah sahib has the white mark on his forehead, will not finish the service of the holy Vishnu for an hour or more. No one will disturb the lady."

An hour or more! The practical soul of the woman of business abhorred the long vacuity; however, she had resources within possible reach. From a capacious pocket she produced some feminine filigree occupation, and ran the ivory bobbin in and out under the vigilant *pince-nez*.

Presently it occurred to her that it might be as well to put together her impressions of the room. A comprehensive glance sufficed. "Plush and broken crockery!" she said, with her characteristic grunt, and as her eyes wandered back to the bobbin, she intercepted the steady scrutiny of a pair of black eyes. They were not by any means a *nice* pair of eyes—long, narrow, a little quizzical, wholly wily and untrustworthy,—hall-marked *spy!* Rebecca Yeastman was certainly not sensitive, or she would have realized earlier that behind almost every curtain lurked some such watcher, soft-footed, noiseless, wakeful. However, this particular inspection in no way disconcerted her—neither annoyance nor curiosity, even of the most fleeting, varied the immobility of her face; and, though she knew it not, it was to this fact that she owed the termination of her vigil. The old harridan, who directed affairs behind the *purdah,* carried back a favourable verdict. "She'll do," she said. "She's as ugly as the toad which croaks in the pond yonder; and she can keep a secret, or may the Gods forever still my lying tongue!"

It was this old woman, Parbathi herself, who went back for her; and she led her through such dark, intentionally devious passages, that Rebecca, though excellent at locality, could never tell whether or not the room she finally entered was in the same building as the one she had left.

The sight which greeted her was sufficiently new and engrossing. The room was large and square with windows too high for purposes of outlook, and closely barred against all use as ventilators. On the floor was a gaudy Western carpet, stamped, literally as well as intrinsically, as cheap German merchandise. In the centre of the room stood a high silver bedstead, hung with opaque curtains, which were evidently not intended as security against mosquitoes, for those musical creatures buzzed among the heavy folds with appreciative contentment. On the floor sat women of varying ages, some shaven and without ornament, others caparisoned gaily enough, all in the rich dark reds and blues of the Kathiawad saree. They were moving their bodies to and fro to a monotonous Gregorian wail, which did not cease for the entrance of the intruder. Parbathi pointed to the bed, and Rebecca approached, being constrained to submit for lack of language, else her initiatory activities would certainly have been devoted to the extrusion of the noise and the introduction of some fresh air.

When her eyes had adapted themselves to the want of light, what she saw in no way alarmed her medical instincts. Among tumbled bedclothes, rich silks, and cheap cotton sheets, lay, fully dressed and bejewelled, a smug, sleek, decently featured Indian lady. Her skin was beautifully smooth, and under her lashes were the accustomed artificial shadows, the material *absit omen* of the nation. One plump hand lay lazily across the clothes, and you saw that the nails were well-kept and dyed with the brilliant *menhdi;* the other hand grasped pettishly the short thick throat.

"Bilious." said Rebecca. Parbathi did not understand, but she saw that the doctor was not impressed by the heinousness of the disease, and she poured out volleys of jargon, waving her hands in wild gesticulation. Then, growing helpless at the sight of Rebecca's calm and sane proceedings,—the matter-of-fact feeling of the pulse, the unceremonious lift of the eye-lid, the business-like production of tablet and pencil for the composition of a suitable tonic—it dawned on her that a communicating tongue was what she wanted; and she darted out to secure old Prabhu Das, the domestic secretary, and the one male, save the Rajah, who was allowed access to this end of the palace. Prabhu Das was just behind the door, watching, and was therefore soon produced. He was a spare, fleshless Hindu, clad in flowing robes over which he wore a long white coat. On his head was a slight black cap, from out which had escaped the wiry grey top-knot, the sign occipital of his Brahminism; and as he bowed and genuflected to the lady, this odd little termination bobbed in the most ludicrous way against the rest of his cleanshaven head. For you must know that Brahmins grow a capillary oasis there alone, where most Westerners are innutritive in old age.

"Your honour," he said, "your Monstrosity, your Magniloquence, learned in the English Aesculapianisms! in this poor house we, prince of the people, are your dusty slaves!"

Here he paused, to leer deprecatingly and express facially his grovelling obsequiousness.

"Humph!" said Rebecca "you know English, I suppose? Well then, this lady has nothing the matter with her which cannot be cured by bestirring herself. She is bilious—that is all—the rest is imagination. Here is a tonic, and I have also noted directions as to diet, air, and exercise. These windows ought to be open, and all these howling women turned out. Do you hear?"

Prabhu Das was the most delightful pantomime possible. There he stood, slightly inclining forward, his hands clasped in agonized supplication, his eyes blinking twenty to the second, and at every few words spoken he jerked his head towards the doctor, opening his mouth in a gape which was meant to convey a combination of assent and astonishment. Then he spoke; the occasion was serious, and his speech matched it.

"Lady not diagnosticate good, right way. Ranee sahib not bile; ranee sahib poison. You see, old Mother Thakrani wear widow's cloth. She cobra-minded, breeze in her brain. She make poison ready. Cook sweetmeats—in sweetmeats hide poison. Ranee eat sweetmeat, now sick, to-morrow die. Rajah sahib carry her on litter, make her ashes. Mother Thakrani too much wicked. Doctor-lady give certificate, write Ranee sahib die poison."

He gasped, exhausted with such direct speaking, for his mind was tortuous.

"Nonsense!" was the retort. "The lady is no more poisoned than I am when I eat too much dinner." But Prabhu Das's next move was more practical. The doctor was presented with a quantity of food, alleged to have been eaten by the Ranee. Neatly bottled was it, and sealed in accordance with local police instructions on the subject—what an amount of study those rules had cost the old man!—And, albeit denying any connection between the food and the royal lady, Rebecca promised to investigate and report the next day. She chuckled gleefully as she carried off her prize; poisons were her special subject, and she had hardly dared to hope that an introduction to the Indian type would be made thus early in her career. The report she wrote before she slept, in the large chandelier-lighted drawing-room of the guest-house.

It was brief enough; the food contained poison sufficient to have extinguished instantly the entire nine lives of the most vital cat. She added an unsolicited rider on the impossibility of the Ranee's having partaken of this—confection, and of the equal absurdity of connecting the thakrani with the deep-laid scheme of which she was suspected.

But the perspicuity of her arguments appealed not to the Darbar. There was poison in the food—so much was certain; therefore the old thakrani (who had not even the most remote connection with the royal kitchen) must be treated as a criminal at the domestic tribunal.

II

Not far from Gower Street station, in a comparatively quiet corner of the city of London, stands a great block of modern red brick. You are back again in the haunts of civilization now, and you press the button to summon the accustomed porter. He comes promptly, and you follow him up a flight of steps, which beam upon you in the unmistakable cleanliness of English soap and water.

"Miss Marion Mainwaring? This way, No. 17,"—says the stout custodian of the Women Students' Chambers, Chenies Street; and he retires with a salute, leaving you to your own resources. *you = english?*

It certainly does look like a student's room, and a woman's—this! Prints of Rubens and Nicolas Poussin, of Cuyp and William Hunt, of Burne-Jones and Rossetti, Madonnas and bacchanal orgies, Dutch sunsets and beggar-boys, hang, in impartial selection and appropriate setting, against the Morris-papered walls. One end of the room is lined with deep-browed tomes, of a scientific and medical aspect; a writing-table in the spacious bow-window betrays an air of recent requisition; softly cushioned lounges invite to unstudious repose; within easy reach are picture-papers and the latest poem. The mantelpiece is laden with the pretty yellow jonquil; and a copper kettle is just beginning to simmer on the pleasantly crackling fire, beside which sits the tall, dark, strong-featured owner of these varied tastes. She reads sheets of closely written foreign paper, and you,—you creep behind her and look over her shoulder.

I

Kathiawad, *November*, 1896

Well, Marion, for all brainless unjust atrocities, commend me to sleek globulous Rajahs of Indian principalities! You will remember the story of the poisoned comfits, and how excited I was at the possibility of investigating an Indian poison so early in my life here? I had such visions of collecting useful *data* for the old octopian in the dear laboratory round which my affections still hover. But, alack, my pride is turned to remorse! The immediate result of my report is that they suspect a poor old widowed ex-queen of an attempt to poison one of her grandson's wives; and she is expelled the palace, bereft of all that might, by any possibility, help her to keep herself in fairly decent comfort elsewhere.

I expect the fact was that the young Ranees disliked the old one, and plotted this device for ridding themselves of her supervision. They tell me she has taken refuge in the house of a former maid, and I mean to go and see her, and hear more of her history.

No! I have not plagued myself with vain regrets, as you'd have done; not, at least, after a quiet sane consideration of the matter. Why should I prick my fingers with the thorns which other people gather? You will know, however, that I did not omit my best persuasions with the prince, useless as I could not help feeling that they were, at the time. Meanwhile to me, personally, the Rajah has been kindness itself. This is only a moderately sized state, and it is not very remarkable for natural or artificial charms.

The country round about is cotton-picking and flat. I rather liked seeing the small sparely clad children (wearing nought but their hair, you know), helping their mothers pick cotton under the bright Indian skies.

But the cotton factories, with their tall unpicturesque chimneys, are an unpleasantly civilized suggestion. Among the arrangements planned for my amusement was a play by a strolling company. The palace has a theatre, but the night was so sultry that the performance transferred itself to an impromptu stage out in the open. It was a strange unforgettable sight, lighted as it was by flaming torches, burning weirdly under the glowering sky. In the foreground sat the Rajah on his gemmed throne, richly jewelled and gaily robed; behind was a throng of fierce black-mustachioed attendants, and closing up round the royal personage an impenetrable guard. Even among his own people he is not safe. They say that at night he sleeps, literally, under drawn swords, two particularly trusty servitors keeping guard, like angels with extended wings, at the head of his bed.

The stage arrangements were rough enough, and the play was, in parts I am told, quite impossible; but ignorance of the language stood me instead of an expurgated edition. It was a pantomimic skit on the administration of justice by the young civilian. A florid Englishman (the mask was really good) sits at a camp-table, holding his migratory court upon a criminal charged with murdering his wife. As he does not yet know the language, he works through an interpreter.

MAGISTRATE. How old was your wife?
CRIMINAL. Ten years.

INTERPRETER. *(fearing that the minority of the victim might heighten the heinousness of the crime, to a civilized mind.)* He says, sir, she was an old woman, of some sixty-five years.

MAGISTRATE. An old woman! Where's the corpse?

INTERPRETER. Now burnt, some twelve months since your Honour's last visit to this Zillah. Prisoner keeping in gaol all the time. But ashes in Prisoner's wallet. Your Honour Inspect?

MAGISTRATE. How old is the Prisoner?

CRIMINAL. Twenty-five years.

INTERPRETER. *(Interpreting again to fit his own ideas of what is best.)* Prisoner same age as late corpse, your Honour, but looking very young. Vishnu—God, salt preserve his life.

MAGISTRATE. *(Whose eyes are opened by this blatant falsehood.)* Hang the man,—to-morrow, five A.M.!

The moral of it all seems to be, when you do stoop to lying, take care that the lies have at least some semblance of plausibility.

The second half of the evening was devoted to conjuring tricks, at which local jugglers are really wonderful. I hear that these jugglers are a caste by themselves, and are a most interesting people, clannish and unapproachable.

To their own caste they are exceedingly kind. A juggler's portionless widow becomes the care of the whole community; his daughters are married at their joint expense, and his sons are taught the trade by the cleverest juggler among them. As a result, the woman is oftenest in best case when widowed. Is it not strange that this should happen in the country where widowhood has always been shown us in the saddest colours? Truly is this a land of anomalies?

But to return: a custom which you would have enjoyed was the evening lamp-lighting. When the sun drops, the torch-bearers congregate at the palace gates, and run in a body, bearing flaring pines in their hands, to salute, at the chief entrance to the palace, the reigning king. He is called by all the titles which his country and the empress bestow upon him, and by all the high-sounding flatteries which the Eastern tongue and loyal subjects can devise. Then the chief torch-bearer lights the lamps in the entrance-hall, till which is done not a single spark must relieve the darkness of the palace. Should there be a prince living in his own separate residence, the ceremony is repeated for him; the same burning pine being carried to light the filial abode! It was all so strange and Oriental, I think it is one of my nicest memories of this place.

I hear that I may visit the old thakrani to-morrow, so you shall have news of her when next I write.

P. S.—What do the ladies do all day, you ask? Quarrel? No, they are too lethargic for any such activity. Most of them turn over and fondle their lovely jewels and silk garments. One Ranee has taken a violent passion for the harmonium. She has dozens of them in all sizes, and by all makers, but refuses to be taught how to handle the instrument in the conventional way. As she is energetic about playing (with one finger and both pedals going furiously!), you can imagine the consequence. I no longer wonder that about half a mile divides the king's apartments from the zenana.

II

KATHIAWAD, *December*, 1896

Oh, my dear Marion, such a hovel it is which houses the poor old thakrani! A great gateway, built for offence and defence does indeed frown threateningly at the public road, and is officered by a custodian equally forbidding and imposing. But, oh! the sordid poverty behind the wicket! Two small rooms are all the house contains. In one live the maid and her family, all devoted to the thakrani, and counting themselves happy to be serving her; the other is at the thakrani's own disposal, but she lives mostly on the little verandah. Here I found her, dressed in a spotless white cloth, seated on the floor, poring with the bedimmed vision of her eighty-four years, over an illumined Sanskrit text. The little gray squirrels ran about her unabashed, hiding in the folds of her draperies, and perching on her shoulder,—a striking contrast! But, ugh!—the mice ran about too, equally privileged, and you will understand how apprehensive these made me feel. In the yard just beyond are tethered the great unsightly buffaloes, and the dwarfed Indian cows, which provide not only the chief food, but also the only income of the small household. The incarnate pathos of it rises to your mind as you look at the old woman. I wish one could help her. She takes things with a large equanimity, however, saying, as they all say in this country, "It is my fate!"

Her jewels have long since been transmuted into coin, one beautiful uncut diamond alone remaining. Should nothing else happen to help her, she will use this to accomplish the final journey of her life. It is such an odd idea. When she feels death near (her horoscope will date the feeling), she will start, however feeble, on a pilgrimage to the sacred Ganges, which is many hundred miles distant from this place. She will take with her the ashes of her son and daughter, having vowed that these should mingle with the sacred fluid.

"If I reach the Ganges," she explained, "after throwing in these two little bags, and saying the necessary prayers, I will lay me down on the bank and die. Sabibree, my faithful maid, will see that all that is necessary is done for my poor frame. This alone is now my care in life."

Of the Rajah she speaks with reluctance. Yet she did tell me how he wrested from her all her possessions, and indeed he still withholds her allowance, month by month, as it falls due, but she is quite sure that, with the gods, there will be retribution for him, and she wastes no human vengeance.

Her ejection from the palace must have been picturesque. It was intended that this should be a final translation; and to this end, with some show of an attempt at reconciliation, was sent her the loveliest of garments. But the old maid, skilled in the poisons of native States, warned her, only just in time, that to wear it would be to prepare her body against cremation. I have a piece of it now, a valued possession. Failing fraud, they had recourse to force. Imagine it all! The breathless, dark night; the swift stealthy steps of the harridan, as she comes to bind her victim, preventing all possible outcry by a tent-peg wedged in between the poor, toothless jaws; the noiseless race (tyranny against helplessness!) through the deserted streets; the secretive palanquin revealing nothing concerning its burden—and, finally the ruthless desertion outside the city gates!

Here she would have fared very badly indeed, but that a kind-hearted palanquin-bearer had given up his place at the poles to the ubiquitous maid, who took her to the house where I found her. . . And to think that all this time the Rajah was entertaining me, to lull my suspicions and keep me off inquiry! I *am* an *oaf*, and could weep with vexation!

III

KATHIAWAD, *May* 1897

Do you remember the old thakrani, and her pitiful story? I have just heard that a few months after I said good-bye to her, she felt the death-call and went her pilgrimage. Her vitality lasted the distance of the sacred river, and she omitted nothing of all she had vowed. But that was a week ago, and she lies in a trance now, on the treeless sand-banks, responsive to neither the fierce sun by day, nor the brilliant stars by night. Can't you see it all? And the eternal river flows by, cold, majestic, unheeding!

Malappa

A Study in Ashes

I had spent a busy morning, and had just driven home with a keen appetite for a late Indian breakfast, when Malappa first summoned me to his presence. His messenger was not prepossessing in appearance, nor indeed did he commend himself to one's too alert olfactory sensibilities; but he was very insistent, and, after all, importunity is still what prevails most with us. So we went, Malappa's *dallal* (broker) on the box. Our destination proved a long row of buildings with a frontage not unworthy a city wall, and a gateway that would have puzzled the besiegers of Lucknow. Crowds of people of all ages and sizes, and apparently (for their speech and dress betrayed them) of every Indian province and nationality, elbowed themselves to the entrance to view us. The situation was unfair—four pairs of eyes against perhaps eight times that number! However, the samples were interesting, and, moreover, were not unwilling to inform us of themselves and their uses in that place. We had come, they said, to the great gathering-place of the faqirs (devotees). It was the property of that particular order of which Malappa was the head, and devotees from the length and breadth of India sojourned there awhile, whenever the service of the gods brought them thitherwards. Presently the messenger returned to conduct us to the presence. We were led through a species of quadrangle, not lawn-kept, but flowering with sacred plants and shrubs. In one corner was a marble canopy overshadowing a platform, on which were displayed rows and rows of neatly arranged deities. A great white Mahdev of ordinary manufacture kept ward over them, these thirty-four gods; and they stood side by side at regular intervals, the whole tale of them, smooth black creatures, varying in size from about four inches to an inch, each god crowned with a pretty, yellow flower. Picturesque *gosains* stood about the garden, in various attitudes of penance, clothed for the most part in oil and paints, their hair in fearful and marvellous condition, and round their necks prayer-necklaces, which any lady might envy for her jewel-casket. As we passed them they cried, "*Defiled, defiled!*" They did not say it at all nastily, but quite pleasantly and benignly, merely as if they were stating a fact for which neither they nor we were responsible.

The house at which our conductor at last halted was rather below the dignity of the gods and the faqirs, and I must own to having felt rather apprehensive when I heard that the next item on our novel programme was the ascent of an appallingly dark staircase—narrower and steeper (I am sure) than the thirty-four little gods' way of salvation.

However, we soon reached the summit, and, when our eyes had adjusted themselves to the light, we discovered—guided by an encouraging voice—a nice old man sitting cross-legged on the floor, very much as nature made him, but for a coating of ashes and white paint laid on in ornamentations and tattooings. This was the great Malappa, chief of the faqirs.

We had to listen first to some graceful apologies. The years sat heavily on this servant of the gods, and stairs were mundanely tiresome; but, having urgent need of our help in some business matter, he had ventured to trouble us thus far. . . etc. etc.

Before Malappa was a small raised stand, on which was placed a tiny baby-god only about half an inch in height. Malappa was doing his private devotions, he said; but he hastened to add that this was no impediment to the free interchange of speech with mortals such as we.

Round about the god were numerous utensils, and pretty little silver *summais* (lamps) with five wicks open to the air (they burn melted butter, not oil, before the gods), and tiny mysterious-looking boxes and trays, to complete the implements of entreaty.

The god (whom Malappa was most kind in expounding) was a pebble found in the river Nerbudda. The faqirs of this order worship only such, and are very proud of the fact that the chisel and hammer are not employed in the divine manufacture. "We fish our gods out of the river," they say; "we do not make them. They create themselves there; and when our stock of gods is exhausted, we go to the Nerbudda for a fresh consignment." The thirty-four gods in the temple were only pebbles in various sizes. We were interested, and begged Malappa to continue his devotions. This he did, without demur. First, the baby-god had his bath; it was rather public, but he did not seem to mind. He was put on a little silver tray, and an ingeniously wrought siphon showered him with pure water, which the faqir had no doubt drawn from some sacred well or spring. When he was judiciously dry (for the weather is rheumatic), he was put on to his tiny stool once more, and the acolytes in attendance opened the pretty boxes and produced some ashes and slimy red and yellow paints, wherewith to anoint him. He was then ready to grant requests. Malappa made them before him for two hours daily, and, when the god got hot and tired over the process, the kind Malappa was always ready to refresh him with a succession of baths and anointings.

Malappa told us in confidence that he was a very powerful kind of god, and would do anything for people who tended him. Mahdev is his name, the Great God,—in the singular number, you will note, albeit he is pleased to multiply himself for the use of individual man,—and his local habitation is this place of ashes. He was most kind to us, and stood aside while Malappa, still cross-legged and still benign, discussed his business with me. Indeed, so little was Mahdev hurt, that, after his own sacred candle had lighted us down the stairs, his ministers followed our retreating steps with the gifts reserved for the saints—a nice hairy cocoanut and a handful of dry dates.

So, back again we went in safety—through the same quiet garden, past the rows of little Mahdevs, and the pilgrims and *gosains* crying as before their pleasant refrain; and, although the great gates of the Place of Ashes did then shut this odd little corner of the world securely from out our commonplace and civilized lives, I still think of the benign Malappa at his daily orisons, making requests in such confident cheerfulness—*dust to dust, ashes to ashes!*

A Living Sacrifice

The Ganges Valley, 1828

N o, I *cannot*, Dwarki!" said little Tani. "I love this present life. I love everything—to watch the gambols of the children and bathe my little Urmi; to sew her small garments, when I am not cooking the dinner or scouring the pans. I love to see the water bubble into the brass vessel as I draw it from the well near the bamboo trees. And it is a joy beyond words when I have dyed my nails the right colour, and donned my brightest garments, and painted the shadows 'neath my eyes—to the intent that she may glare with envy—Gunga of the unlucky foot, whose heart is burnt as dry as babul firewood. And must all this come to an end? No more gambols or gay jewels or even household duties; no more victories over the less fortunate! No! *No!* I *cannot!*"

THE SISTERS STOOD HAND IN hand, duplicates past all identification in height and feature and appearance. "Never were twins so alike," said the villagers. But in character and expression a world of difference lay between them, for the close observer. Dwarki was the wife of a man serving a long sentence in the Andamans for complicity in some daring dacoity. She had barely seen him, indeed, for she was but a child when he was banished, and her life had been one uncomplaining service of her sister, and of Chandri, her sister's exacting mother-in-law.

Chandri had given her a home when the sentence which carried the son across the "black waters" had also proved to be, for the feeble old mother, the decree peremptory for a transportation which knows no periods. And Dwarki was not allowed to forget the kindness.

Only this morning had Chandri recapitulated the fact, with many annotations, as to the straits to which an extra mouth reduced one's larder (yet with no acknowledgment of the advantages of a willing and efficient pair of extra hands!), and, having worked herself into her most self-complacent querulousness, she had set off for a day at the village fair.

"I may stay the night," she had called back, as the grove of mango trees hid her bundle and stick and shining brass *lota* from view.

"The gods grant it!" had rejoined, under their breath, the two maidens.

And now it was dusk, and the sisters stood hand in hand, with Tani's husband lying a stiff, still mass on the *charpai* at their feet. He had stumbled in from his work. "Pray to Kali," said he; "the sickness is upon me!"

And, though there was no unfaithfulness as to either prayers or remedies, he had soon writhed himself into an eternal quietude. How his silent presence filled the room! There was no escaping it! And at dawn the neighbors would carry him to the burning ground by the sacred river, and little warm, living, quivering Tani must be bound to the cold dead form in order that the yellow fire might purify them both.

"I cannot! I *cannot!*" she repeated.

"Heart of me!" said Dwarki, "I would I had your chance. To buy immortality for a husband, is not this the crown of life, the bliss of death! Think what might have been, had the gods taken you first, in the way of other mortals. Or, look indeed at me, without husband or child, and he to whom I am bound toiling in chains, or maybe dead, unblest! Who knoweth?"

"No! *No! I cannot* do it!" moaned Tani. "It is impossible. Dost remember the day when I caught the bit of live firewood in my two hands? Hi! how it burnt. I feel the pain now. No doubt, this ill luck cometh through the evil eye of that Gunga. For did she not crow, 'You should make better acquaintance with the fire, for the sake of the inevitable final salutation.' How knew she that it would claim me, *living! . . . Living! . . .* Oh no! Dwarki, show me a way of escape. Never have you failed me before. Save me now, as you love me. The mother-in-law is, happily, away. Let us hide ourselves, you and I, somewhere—in the long grass by the river, maybe, or in the fields of sugar-cane—till we escape to the mountains. Come soon, *soon,* ere the neighbors know. *He* will get attention. . . no need to think of that; and I have left him a son, for future priestly offices. Oh, come! *Come!*"

"Poor child!" said her sister; and, gathering her into her arms, she soothed and loved her. "I would this might be spared you, an you dread it so. See! we need not let the villagers know just yet; rest you awhile, while I go to the temple in the grove and pray guidance of the gods. Perchance a way will be found. Besides, there is the mango bough, which the woods must yield us; we may not omit that first act of widowhood, whatever follows. Then are there certain purchases to be made also."

"Let me come with you," said Tani; "the children sleep soundly." So, putting the quaint old puzzle-padlock on the outer door they sallied forth.

The wayside grocer met their temporal needs—clarified butter ladled from the earthenware pot, into Dwarki's brass *lota,* with a liberal supply of red *kunkun.* To this she added a ball of black opium. Opium is useful, on occasions. *real*

And now they were once more within the house of mourning.

"Did the holy bull show you a way?" asked Tani eagerly.

"Yes!" was Dwarki's reply, with grave, determined face. "Eat first, my sister; the rest will appear presently. The impending journey absolves us from our fast."

And the ball of black opium lay within the only cake of grain-flour to which Tani's indifferent appetite could be tempted.

"Hi! hi! Death visits me, luckless!"

The melancholy chant rang out on the night air, entering each open door, a personal summons to the house of mourning. One and another stopped her evening avocation, and followed the sound with rapid footsteps, till quite a little crowd had gathered about the home of the twins. Beside the dead sat Dwarki, clasping to her breast that broken bough, sign picturesque of her broken life. The women tried to elicit from her the manner of his death; but she shook her head, too overpowered for more than "Kali was merciless!" (Might not her voice betray her!)

"Ah!" said they, "the cholera! luckless fate!" and the elder women fell to preparing the preliminary rites and anointings—("Let her cry, poor child!"),—while those with voices ranged themselves in rows facing each other, to sing the death-wail. Dwarki rocked herself to and fro, joining only in the regularly recurring "*Oh! oh! oh! oh!*"—chromatic chorus of sorrow.

"Where was Dwarki?" asked one suddenly.

"Gone with the mother to the fair!" was the mendacious answer.

It was the dead man's brother, after all, who bore the pan of incense, swinging it to and fro as he headed the procession, keeping time to the tread of the burden-bearers and the song of the women.

He had come in at daybreak from the neighboring village, with the news that the old mother had been run over by a cart at the fair and could not travel for many days. Little knew he for what sacred office he was only just in time. Behind him came the leading men of the caste-brotherhood, and the litter strewn with bright pink roses over the rough cotton pall. Dwarki walked immediately behind, in a phalanx of singing women, and holding in either hand the fatherless children, round-eyed and frightened.

And, all this time, the real widow lay opium-drugged in the safely remote storeroom of the little establishment!

THEY HAVE NOW REACHED THE bank of the sacred stream, and the drum is sounding the suttee proclamation.

The brother produces a pot of clarified butter and a pan of red *kunkun,* and, with the help of the village headman, bathes and anoints the dead body, robing it in fresh white garments. And the priests stand by, forgetful already of the present, praying for a dignified rendering of the immediate outcome!

Meanwhile the altar is in preparation—an arrangement of stakes, covered with things combustible, dry faggots, and leaves which blush red for shame at the uses to which men put them; the silken hemp and the fibre of the cocoanut, with an overpouring of oil and butter.

Of Dwarki the women have taken charge. She too has bathed for the last time in the sacred water, and wears the white garments of the devotee, with her *obolus* for Charon (parched rice and cowries) tied securely into one corner. To the barber belongs the right of painting the sides of her feet with red *kunkun:* none who bear that mark may withdraw the gift of themselves from the altar.

In the midst of her friends she stands, and unclasps one by one her ornaments. "Keep that necklace, Kashi. And you, Kamala, these anklets. Ofttimes have they tinkled accompaniment to our chatter, as we drew our morning bucket of water in glad companionship. This locket to my best friend. It bears my name, and my horoscopical charm. The gods grant it bring you luck! To me has none ever come! "

Her marriage bangles she broke—final attestation of widowhood—and a shudder ran through the poor girl's frame. For the first time it occurred to her that she might be tempting the gods to make her a widow in truth. Was she imperilling the life of the convict? Too late to retract now.

"Of what art thou thinking, oh bereaved one?" said the veteran matron in the group. "Put out thine hands!" And round each small wrist was bound the red cord of sacrifice. "Now greet thy children quickly; the priest awaits thee!"

"God bless you both!" said Dwarki. And, in a whisper: "Tell Tani that I loved to die; it was release. I knew no fear. Canst remember that, boy? "

"Yes! yes!" he said, repeating the message. "Love and death, and no fear!"

"Art ready, oh bereaved?" was calling the priest. "The sacred circle is formed."

Drawing her widow's raiment closer about her, Dwarki spread out the overhanging end to receive the measure of rice which was to be distributed to the assembly.

"Three times round the circle, remember," said the priest. And she walked slowly round, putting into each outstretched hand a few grains. "God has bereaved me," it meant; "for you may there be plenty!"

In the bungalow by the water-gate lived the engineer sahib; and seeing the crowd he walked to the water's edge. He arrived in time for the largess. As he put out his hand, "Lady of sorrow!" said he, speaking in her own tongue, "if you wish to escape this ghastly exaction, I and my household are at your service. I have but to call, and from the garden yonder will come men sufficient in number to effect your rescue."

She smiled her gratitude, but shook her head.

"Think on this thing," said he. "Do not your children need you? Tell me your decision at the next round."

But when she did again approach him, the sad little negative was still her only answer.

"There is yet time to reflect," said the Western; "I await the final round."

"The Moving Finger has written that this should be," was all it brought him. And the man turned sadly away: further interference was impossible.

On the altar lay the victim of the gods; round the altar walked the victim of the priests, scattering parched rice and cowries—(cowries are legal tender in the shades!).

"Odd!" she was saying in her mind, "the seven steps of mine own marriage I never took, but the gods are accepting from me the seven steps which belong of right to someone else's funeral. "

They bound her to *the burden* on the altar—the sweet smell of the incense perfuming the air, and the villagers standing awed and silent. From the muddy depths of the sacred water a crocodile raised an inquisitive head, and the frogs croaked comment satisfactory. As far as eye could see stretched the featureless sand-banks, with here and there a line of dreary babuls. A pipal tree once tried to grow by the suttee stone, but a blast of lightning had reduced it to what seemed like an epitome of the tragedy which it had so often witnessed.

CORNELIA SORABJI

"Hist!" said an attendant to his fellow. "Hoist up those bambus, one on each shoulder, *so*—ere the ropes be tightened."

But he paused—the shiny yellow things in the air; for the crowd had parted to admit a flying figure—Tani, but just awakened from her drug-induced slumbers,—horror, and yet relief, following upon comprehension as. she glanced wildly round her.

"My sister!" she shrieked beside the motionless form.

Dwarki had closed her eyes in the quivering shudder of the awful contact; but she opened them once more on God's sky and on that piteous little face so close to hers. And as the bambus were gently lifted into place, and the ropes bound about her, she smiled a humorous smile.

"Almost was that drug a waste!" she reflected.

For Tani had accepted the sacrifice!

The Fire is Quenched!

A Sketch in Indian Ink

I

(*Introductory Note.*—Under the early Zoroastrian law, contact with a dead body meant contamination, for which the penalty was ten thousand stripes, *i.e.* death.

The Zoroastrian idea of worship lies in keeping the sacred fire perpetually alight on the altar. It must never be allowed to go out. There is no greater sin than neglect of this duty.)

The town was ecclesiastical—of this there was no doubt. It was not your peculiar faculty for seeing which disclosed this to you,—indeed you have yet all to learn concerning this special kind of ecclesiasticity,—but there was an air of quiet, hushed sanctity abroad, which somehow thrust the conviction upon you.

It is picturesque type of sanctity, too. The hour is six in the evening. Look at the women, sitting with their faces west-wards, weaving, weaving, and praying silently the while. They are all daughters and wives of the priesthood; and those pretty and costly silk draperies would be becoming, you reflect, to faces even less pleasing and cultured than those which meet your eye. The head is bound with a white fillet, typical of the subjection of all actions and imaginings to the bondage of the law; and among the draperies is visible a finely embroidered white lappet—a garment every square inch of which has some religious significance. . . But the women weave and weave; and it looks so uninteresting this thing which they weave:—neither the soft delicate-tinted silk, nor even the white linen embroidery, but just lengths of cord no thicker than ordinary packing twine. It is the Zoroastrian *kusthi*, the sacred cord: there are seventy-two gossamer-like strands woven into it—seventy two, for the seventy-two angels; and as she weaves, the good Zoroastrian lady will say prayers for all the future generations who may use that sacred *kusthi*. One day it will pass through the fingers of some pretty, careless girl, or maybe a feather-headed boy, who will tie the knots with flippancy and reel off the ancient zend in meaningless levity. But, and if the weaver be but faithful enough, perhaps those incessant short prayers of hers will act as a charm against all future contingencies.

"That I shall ask Thee, tell it me right, O Ahura!

"How arose this present life?

"By what means are the present things to be supported?

"O righteous Mazda! Be their guardian, to ward off from them every evil: Thou art the promoter of all life.

"In every being which beholds the sun's light, may Armaiti, the spirit of piety, reside.

"The good of the good mind is in Thy own possession, O righteous!

"The voice of the law, it is *Thy* voice, O Ahura Mazda!"

Thus spake old Avemai, as she bends to her task in the open doorway of the high priest's house. She is worn with years and with disappointed hopes—a little crooked old woman, but with character and determination proclaiming itself from every furrow of the wrinkled face.

Khursud, the high priest, is her son, and she lives with him and his pretty wife Makkhi in the house which had been his father's and grandfather's before him. At this stage of existence her affections are busy over little Khutti, aged five, the grandchild. Such a winsome child it is, too—the most delicate of limbs, dark brown curls, and eyes to match, and a mouth made for laughter. Listen! you can hear a little joyous peal this very minute. Khutti drives her goat-cart home from the pleasure-house by the water; and Siddi, the small negro attendant, has been acting zany for her amusement.

"Do it again, Siddi," she says, "and again. Show me how the big fish eat the little fish, and how it slipper-slippered down his throat."

"I can do better than that," said Siddi; "I can show you how a fish can slipper-slipper down Siddi's own throat. But that will be another day, after I have had a chance of dodging that long-limbed old cook in his hot-weather garment. This evening you shall hear all about why your grand-aunts send you so many fish—big and little—on your birthdays; and why the mai, who sweeps the house, paints them, the lucky things, all over the doorsteps and pavement; and why in short, a fish always means that good things will happen."

And so he told her, in his own whimsical way, a legend of his own devising—touching the Parsee exodus from Persia, and how when mermaids and devils would have tempted the exiles out of their course, a great scaly fish with a waving tail, swam before them, to land them, and the sacred fire they guarded, with due safety in their Indian refuge.

And when it was ended—"There! isn't that pretty?" said he. "But here is the scolding ayah. I must get beyond reach of her bangle-laden arm!"

"Eh! Siddi! Ever filling my baby's ears with infidel tales. *Pshu!*—begone, I say. I will tell the bai sahib of you some day."

"Oh, ayah!" said Khutti, "he has told me lovely tales, about fishes, and things in the sea, and big ships."

"Pooh! lies, lies, all lies! Son he is of a sow-eared mother," replied the woman. "Yes! Makkhi bai sahib—baby coming to supper and bed."

Through the hot hours of the next day Khutti played in her luxurious little nursery, requisitioning whatever playmate her imperious fancy suggested, and always setting the right one too—solemn father, or bonny mother, or fond, wrinkled old grandame.

And she told them all her fish story, and they had to act and react it a hundred times: now she was the smiling maiden, and now the red coral gnome, and now again the great big fish with his leering slit of a mouth and winking eye.

But, after her usual evening drive, she sought the old Ave, once more at her accustomed weaving, and—"Oh, Avemai," she said, "my throat here, it hurts so." No one knew how it happened—a bad drain, perhaps a little cold. Who could tell? Ayah said Siddi had bewitched her; and Siddi was tied up and whipped, in the servants' regions, and made to go through the most gruesome of ordeals, although indeed he barely felt the pain of the lash as he sobbed his small heart out for grief that his little mistress was ill.

But neither this, nor the spells of any caste, or class, or religion, worked the longed-for improvement. And at last—it was but a chance—"Take her to the hills," said the doctor; "the fever may abate, at any rate."

II

IT WAS FIVE IN THE morning at a quiet Indian railway station. The booking-clerk was asleep—the full length of him—on the table in the office, with a red-and-green woollen comforter round his neck, his official cap neglected on the dusty floor, and over his legs loose white folds of quasi-petticoat, which, with his imitation English coat, gave him a strangely hybrid appearance.

CORNELIA SORABJI

"Ding, dong! ding, dong! ding, dong! Train left last station," shouted the porter, thrusting a drowsy head momentarily into the booking-office. The clerk rose and yawned, and cracked the knuckles of his bony fingers, and proceeded to deal little green tickets to the greasy crowd behind the railing. Applicants there were of every description—applicants with bundles on their heads or their backs, and with ten days' provisions in their wallets. Sometimes the bundles were heard to scream—human screams; and often they were seen moving recalcitrant little limbs. (To carry a baby in a sling over your shoulder is a favourite Eastern device.) Of licensed vendors at this early hour there were but few; but the lean hungry Brahmin priest, with his collecting-box, "For the preservation of the Cow," and his bribe of cut flowers, was already walking the platform, and small boys carrying unappetising trays of sickly Indian sweetmeats were being patronized at the third-class compartments, while the messman's assistant made his customary proffer of tea and coffee.

From a luxuriously reserved carriage issued a Parsee lady, dressed in pale blue silk draperies, falling gracefully into the lines of her slight figure; in her arms she carried a child loosely clad in a red crimson vest—the rich colour whereof lighted up the little face. And it needed that; for, notwithstanding the slight smile about the lips, its suggestion of stillness, somehow, struck a cold chill to your heart.

Servants, of varying degree, were in attendance—offering garrulous and obtrusive aid; but the lady refused to be relieved. "A carriage, Marothi, quick!" she commanded; "and bid them drive to the kitchen door. The household is not to be disturbed."

Arrived unobserved at baby's nursery, Makkhi—for it was she, the mother of the erstwhile joyous little Khutti—barred the door, and flew instantly across to the dawning light at the window.

"They must never know that she died in the train," she reflected, "and in my arms too, poor darling! The grandame would say 'twas contamination. What is the penalty? Beating with ten thousand stripes! Ah! It would mean death. And yet, without my Khutti, what care I for life? But—and I must be sadly callous—my heart is like the marble stone on which I shall soon lay her. Not a tear can I shed. It is well, perhaps; no time is there for weeping. I must lay my plans. . . Even ayah fancies she is asleep. Well! in half an hour I must send for the dying-slab, and lift her on to it. My grief will be sufficient excuse for the barred door. At eight, when the granny is through her usual duties,

I will bring her in and show her the cold little body. Oh! that I could warm it! Khutti mai—wake up! wake up!" she wailed, clasping the little thing tight against her own warm breast, a world of yearning in her voice and attitude.

Oh! irrevocable death!

Meantime Ave had been very busy. It was her husband's "*day*"—the anniversary of his death, and there were special dishes to be cooked, and there was his room claiming attention. Daily through the long years since his bones had dropped through the grid, in the Tower of Silence, had provision been made for the possible wants of his spirit: fresh changes of raiment were placed ready for him, and his favourite dishes, and the little snuff-box handy on the arm of his long chair. The snuff never diminished, and the clothes looked strangely unrumpled, and there was no perceptible difference under the covers—but spirits have odd ways. Perchance were the things not there, he would miss them.

On his great day Avemai came herself to look after the arrangements; his fullest priest's robe it must be to-day, and that conical white hat, and the most elaborate of his sandals. She was so particular about everything that it was quite eight o'clock before she encountered ayah. She was on her way to the wine-cellar to get a bottle of the oldest brew—for in those good days bottles of wine were buried at the birth of each child in a Parsee household, giving quite respectable antiquity to the consumable fluid in the cellars of some of the old families. She encountered ayah then—and "You here!" she said. "You have startled me! Have you returned for aught?"

"Khutti mai got worse," said the woman; "the bai sahib brought her home. She is mad with grief. I have sent for the doctor sahib; and the bai has locked the baby's door, and watches the child on the dying slab."

"Fool!" said the old woman. "Why did you not call me?"

"Who bade me call you?" queried the menial, with the irresponsibility of the Indian servant.

Ave hurried, with tottering steps, to the nursery door. "Mi! Mai! Makkhi mai! let me in," she said—and could say no more.

But the door was ajar, and there was Makkhi at a discreet distance from the little dead form on the cold white marble. But the tension had snapped in the still solitude of the death-watch, and she was sobbing now, sobbing healing tears.

"No," thought Ave. "I may not even touch the child, to test the truth of what I see. The bearers must do the final rites."

IT WAS THE WEAVING HOUR, when a long white-robed procession of high priests and priests of lower degree, walking two abreast—a spotless handkerchief unfolded between each pair—followed, in silence, the death-bearers to the distant Tower of Silence. Something there was, not altogether without hope, in the absence of the solemn black, which is the outward and visible sign of Western mourning. Yes! not without hope—albeit the death-bearers must mount alone the steps to those high shelves in the turret, and leave there the dainty little burden to the rough talons and sharp beaks of the hungry vultures.

And, at home, Ave wept bitter tears into the names of the seventy-two angels—(for nothing excused that sunset duty)—and the wives of the white-robed mourners sat in long rows on the verandahs, and chatted nothings or tactless somethings to the broken-hearted mother.

III

MIDNIGHT, AND A BRIGHT MOON overhead. Makkhi has had a wretched evening, sleepless and anxious, and aching with longing for the impossible; and, at last, she has crept noiselessly to the darkest corner of the fire temple. There is Khursud, her husband, reciting the classic zend, in his monotonous voice. Distinctly came the words of the old Gatha.

"I ask from Thee, O Homa! who expellest death, that I may stand forth at will, powerful and successful upon earth; putting down trouble and annihilating the destructive powers. I ask from Thee, Homa! who expellest death, who grantest strength and vigour to those who, mounted on white horses, run in the race—I ask that I may stand forth as victor and conqueror in the battle upon earth. Strike a deadly blow, O yellow Homa, at the body of the disturber of righteousness, who binds our thoughts to earth and earthly things, and makes us forget the sacred religion of Zarthushta. Strike the blow, O yellow Homa! Strike!"

How he had loved the child! And this duty, keeping the fire alight—must it not weigh on his soul tonight? Yet he did it! Ah! they knew how to cling to duty, those two—Khursud and his old mother—and they clung fiercely, as if in that alone lay life, salvation.

Could she tell them? And if not she, who would? It was her own secret, whispered a voice within. Even the doctor had not been in time, and there was no one to suggest the hour at which death had in reality supervened.

But to keep a secret, how impossible! And a secret of her own wickedness, too! Ah! she must speak, if she would buy peace of mind and strength to live.

They were loving too, those two—so tenderly loving—perhaps they would show her how to expiate; and, at worst, 'twas only Death which could come. . . Besides, it was her duty to tell. This last was the thought which would recur most often with the memory of Ave and her weaving at her heart, and with the sight of Khursud burning the sacred sandalwood before her eyes in stern unmovedness.

But she was so young, and life was still sweet, and the love of her husband sweeter still—how could she confess! No, let her have time to think. So it prolonged itself—the struggle—for a succession of nights; the fiercest part of the battle always fought in the far corner of the fire temple—and the result always problematical. Till—the merest chance brought decision. The evening and the morning were the seventh day; and Khursud, walking the empty room at the close of his nightly vigil, found, to his surprise, Makkhi lying against a stone pillar, asleep through sheer watching and fatigue,—while she, startled past discretion, and touched by his kind thoughtfulness for her, obeyed her best impulse, and told him all.

There never was any doubt as to the sequel. Ave issued the mandate. The book said ten thousand stripes; ten thousand—be it. . . and Khursud must administer them.

IV

It is midnight once more; but the moon has veiled her light, as it were in pity for the cruelties of good men's tender mercies.

There is silence, the silence of expectation, in the long, low fire temple; the faint sweet odour of burning sandalwood is in the air; the red light glows on the altar. Is it the only live thing within the walls? Presently the priest's private door opens noiselessly, and there enter together the little, old, bent Avemai, the stern embodiment of the Zoroastrian Leviticus, and (picturesque foil!) the young pathetic-faced mother—beautiful, but still criminal—criminal, because she loved much; because the mother's heart in her would not let the dying child smile its last smile into a strange face; because, as long as the world lasts, the voice of ignorant man will always outshout the inspirations of the all-knowing God.

CORNELIA SORABJI

At a little distance behind the women followed Khursud, the high priest. His spotless robes carried the suggestion of something awful and unapproachable; and yet, did he raise that bent head of his, you would see that he was only a poor crushed creature, not intoxicated by a sense of duty, like his stern old mother—conscious but that his loved child was where the vultures were gathered together, and that the only thing which made life livable would soon be there also. Self-despoiled! childless! wifeless! inexorable fate! Truly was the law his taskmaster!—but to bring him, where? to what?

Then spoke old Avé, the daughter, the wife, the mother of the Zoroastrian priesthood. "My son! that which thou hast to do should be done quickly! and it should be done here, before the altar. Let the Holy Prophet know 'tis done in his name. Bare thy back, my Makkhi. I have loved thee much; but we must all perforce love the law and the prophet more. To this end were we born, and to prove this have I tarried on earth so long. . . Here is the lash: *ten thousand stripes*, says the book. Perhaps—fewer. . . will. . . suffice."

An owl screeched in the cocoanut palms. "Ha!" thought Khursud, "how my pretty Khutti used to shudder at that noise." Then, oddly enough—"The cocoanuts will be ready for tapping this month. Shall we go and drink an early glass of the sweet white juice at the palm groves by the sea? Makkhi, *little* Makkhi! what was it you wore the day we exchanged the betrothal ring? . . . Good God! *I can't!*"

"Come, Khursud," said the unwavering voice of the law. "She is ready *now!* . . . The wisdom of the prophet must be justified of her children."

THE OLD WOMAN LAY ON her face, beseeching GOD—(not the fire, nor the seventy-two angels, nor yet even Zoroaster himself this time; she wanted something, someone, beyond and above these)—beseeching GOD with all the powers of her lean, limited soul to accept this expiation—to send the pain be not very great—oh! to interpose, to end it all, *somehow.*

ONE, . . . TWO, . . . THREE, . . . they came unflinchingly; the lash rising and falling on the silent night air. How the long minutes passed they knew not, and no one counted the strokes—till—

"My son! my son! the fire on the altar, it is dead! *dead!* DEAD! and for the first time since our fathers brought it across the waters! Oh! who will expiate *now*? We have punished the lesser sin—but the greater?"—

So spoke Ave, at sight of the neglected altar; there followed once more a silence, and once more 'twas broken by a shriek—but a shriek piercing and awful in its hopeless unrelievable horror. And this time it came not from the owl in the palm tree.

The law of Zoroaster, the wisdom of the prophet, is she justified of her children—now?

ACHTHAR

The Story of a Queen

H ave ye not exacted enough of me, O Gods? And now my revenge is accomplished, and my vow kept, may not I have back the use of this poor left arm? Selfish Deity! long enough has it been upraised to thee. Well, 'twas writ as my fate."

Thus Rukhi—and she turned to abuse her clumsy little handmaiden for overboiling the rice and overbaking the coarse rye bread, for not tethering the donkey, and for breaking a new pot of spring water. She was a miserable figure enough to look upon, wizened and hideous, and, though scarce seventy, as sapless as that dead old banian tree across the road. And if you would know her history, you have but to walk a step farther to the village over against her sparsely thatched hut. The villagers are just about gathering round the pipal tree for their evening smoke; seek them there.

"What! a stranger wanting a light. Yes, Mahadeo will strike you one with his sharp flints. And—a pot of *jagri* and tobacco-leaves, did you say? Most travellers do not carry so much. In that case sit beside our patel: he loves a *huqqa*."

The *huqqas* are gurgling contentedly now, and being in a mood for it, the patel repeats the oft-told tale. What will he not do for a man who has brought him his favourite decoction?

"You must know, then," he said, "that my story is of a time when I ran about the streets owning nothing, absolutely, in the whole world beyond the sacred thread which was round my waist, and a little talisman which someone had put round my neck at my birth. This alone will show you how long ago it must have been; but—if you wish to fix the time another way, the Peishwa was then fearing a fight with 'the people of the hat' from the little island in the far country, and the princes of Satara were killing each other about the succession to the *gaddi*. In our Rajasthan, also, confusion threatened. You have heard of Rajah Futeesingh, the Sadhu? He was beautiful as a lotus, beloved of Krishna, with the attributes of a god (all except vengeance—to that, poor man! he never attained). He had been reigning some years; but though no less than four successive wives had been carried to the burning-ground out yonder by the river, no heir was left to his house, and his cunning, fiery, evil brother Hari would have the throne when the wood was bound to his own poor body. His mother often brooded upon this. It was very sad; she loved her firstborn; moreover, she feared also—she feared her dead husband's wrath. Hari would say no prayers for his soul, Hari would not pay his debts. What would her second genesis be if all this were left undone? No! the gods must help her out of the difficulty. So, when her astrologers and various inauspicious little incidents would allow, she went in to her good son, the king, and, bowing low before him, she blessed him to the sixth generation of his antecedents; she tied a peacock's feather round his left wrist; she anointed his eyes with some greasy black mixture, as in the days when she carried him slung across her back; she cursed his brother, her son (he was 'the offspring of a donkey,' 'an eater of hog's flesh,' 'a companion of *dheds*,' . . . and other interesting and authentic items); she stroked the king's head, and cracked all her ten fingers against her own temples. Then taking up her small cruse of oil, and having assured herself of the chains of heavy gold round her neck and arms, she went forth on a long self-appointed pilgrimage to Mathura.

"The priests along the way had much advice to give, terminating always in a divorce from one of her rich ornaments, and a promise of greater blessings on some future equally Midasian journey; but at length she found a counsellor less interested than the rest. 'Do not waste more time,' he said; 'The gods love sacrifices—but to *themselves*, not to the priests. Go home at once. Near the sea, about six *kös* from the palace, where the palms rise straight against the red evening sky, and close by the white and gilded temple of the god Gunpathi, you will find a lovely tree, destined by the gods for this high purpose. It flowers plenteously, and is beautiful to look upon. Take your son forth as if to meet a bride, and celebrate his marriage with this holy tree. It will break the evil spell. But omit no portion of the true ceremony as performed by faithful Brahmins. And may Krishna send you your heart's desire!'

"The poor loving soul was home again in due time, and in excellent spirits. The journey had been long, and the snows lay somewhat heavier than of yore about her temples, and perhaps her back was a trifle less erect; and her hand trembled as she held the cup of sweet cold water which the king hastened to offer her. But what did anything matter? All would now be well with him, before she died, and she would see her son's son, and peace upon the house of Futeesingh. So the arrangements were

CORNELIA SORABJI

made with alarming speed. No! they would wait for nothing, not even for the marriage-month. And soon Futeesingh was riding home on a gay red-and-yellow caparisoned elephant, with the bridal wreath round his neck and the *kunkun* on his forehead. The villagers had sneered a little at first; but there was that about the king and his regal old mother which somehow silenced sneers, and there were such rejoicings and gay doings as had never been before in all the land.

"Now you must know that just at the corner of the road, opposite the fifth shrine on the way to the palace, was the house of Premshanker, the great banker. Rukhi, the old woman you saw, was his wife, and she lived there with Achthar, a beautiful girl, betrothed, they said, to Nilkanth, her son. But Nilkanth had gone away, when quite little, with his father to Calcutta, and years had elapsed, and the seven steps were not taken, and Achthar was growing a great girl, and her friends scoffed at her for not owning pots and pans of her own, and for not having a 'lord' to worship. To-day was Ganesh Chathurthi, and as her lusty old mother-in-law had gone to a neighbour's for a gossip and a glimpse of the mad marriage, Achthar was left to her own resources.

"'*You* had better not look on at the wedding,' had sneered Rukhi; 'I should say you were as unlucky as a widow'—and she laughed a mirthless, fiendish laugh.

"Poor little Achthar! Yes, it was true; she knew it. Did not her best friend, Vidya, ask her to hide herself when she should ride out of the town with her bridegroom to Indore? And had they not, in fact, delayed their journey a whole day because Vidya's eyes had rested on Achthar as she carried her morning pitcher to the well in the square? But, for the first time she was angry with Fate for this ill-treatment. Was she no better than that mangy yellow cat, who had similarly hindered Kamala's marriage?

"It was cruel indeed! *Why* had they married her to the boy who never came back to her? And it was Rukhi's boy; why did Rukhi scold her for his absence? But a consolatory thought soon came. It was Ganesh Chathurthi, and there was Ganpat, the oily red little god in the white hole across the road. All her friends were praying to him to-day. The little children with no husbands prayed for good ones, and the married women with bad husbands prayed for better ones in another birth. She would go, too, and pray for something. The god would understand, perhaps, when she told him all about it; and then, too, she might see the wedding procession as it passed by. No one would notice her; and she had not the insignia of widowhood—no bare arms, no close-shaven head—*not yet*. There could be no harm in it. So without further thought she filled her hand with rice from the black pot on the shelf, and ran across to pay her visit to Ganpat. He was smiling blandly under the red paint, and the oil made him look quite nice and melting. She was sure he would bring matters to some crisis, and—there was the noise of the wedding—he must guess all; she could not spare time to tell him. 'There! take the rice, good Ganpat.' What numbers of outriders! And is that the king? Ah! how handsome! *He* was a god, not Ganpat, the red, oily thing. But in her eagerness she had crept outside the shrine, and stood by the roadside, looking straight at the king. And now, alas! one of the torchbearers who ran by his side saw and knew her.

"'Ho! what do you here, inauspicious one, worse than widow? Would you bring curses on our king?'

"But poor Achthar, precipitate with fright and confusion, had run right across the path of the lordly elephant—and oh! she had not seen that huge stone. The crowd was breathless. Of course 'Bhiku,' the fiercest of the king's elephants, would trample her to death. Awful omen! But, wonderful to tell, in a second the soft, white, cloudy mass was lifted up in his trunk, and—what presumption!—'Bhiku' had tossed her on to the king's lap. Did he look angry? No one can ever tell, for the evening was drawing in, and she, poor little girl! was saved embarrassment by a lapse to unconsciousness. Anyhow, the king would not have her removed, and they rode so, straight to the palace gates. They made individual reflections on the incident, you may be sure.

"'The gods gave her to you,' said the enraptured mother.

"'She belongs to me,' said the king.

"'The god heard the prayer I never said,' murmured little Achthar to herself in an ecstasy of joy, as she lay quite still on the yellow silk cushions in the west hall, and watched the sun setting without, and thought on all that that kind old lady had told her, as she bathed her temples. She quite forgot it would mean being a queen; she had room for nothing but a certain vision of large, deep, dark eyes, which reached some hidden feeling within her, and made her thrill at the very memory. . . Well, you have guessed the rest—there was another and a real wedding this time. Of course there were preliminaries to arrange. Achthar was betrothed, as I have said, and her husband must be eliminated before they could do anything. The king's mother arranged that. We never knew how, but word came that he had been concerned in some great forgery case, of which all the world has heard, about one Nuncoomar, in the North. The police could tell you more; the particular ones who witnessed against him retired soon after, and are now very rich, and settled in Lahore. You might ask them about it; and the judge, perhaps, would give you his notes of the case. He must know what sin Nilkanth committed. Rukhi, his mother, was frenzied with rage as she put a torch to the bright brass *summai* after her eventful absence; but her only redress lay in revenge. So she shut up her great house, and built herself the little hut which you saw—built it of dried palm-leaves and straw and huge bambus, and she went on a visit to a *gosain* who lives in the next village, who initiated her into vows of vengeance. The ceremony was revolting, as was Rukhi's life from that day. She walked back to her hut with ashes on her head and her left arm erect, and it has never been down since. She vowed she would keep it there till she had had her revenge. But the gods do not understand a limit: it is withered and stiff still, and will not move, even though her vengeance has slumbered peacefully this long time. When you come to think of it, there is something to admire in her gigantic and determined will—and she was a clever woman in her time, old Rukhi. I was afraid of her as a boy. I had been stealing grain in a shed behind her hut one day, and I saw—ugh! the hideous sight—I saw her drink the blood of a young goat, and I heard her vow the most awful retribution; and then she boiled the tail of a newt, and the forefeet of lizards, and the eyes of an owl, in her huge cauldron, and she muttered curses on the king and his lovely bride; and on the dear little prince whom the gods sent them. I doubt whether she could have done any harm to the great folk at the Rajmahal had not the king's younger brother helped her. He hated them too, of course; and people with a common purpose somehow find each other out. It was on the prince's first birthday; the king had organised a great commemorative hunt, and Hari lost his way coming home. He stumbled towards the only light he could see before him—the darkness falls rapidly on our forests, you must know. It was in old Rukhi's hut. She was nearly mad by this time, and went on muttering, regardless of the stranger filling her narrow doorway. But he had heard enough to make him her ally. After that, Hari often found his way to the ugly old witch when everyone was asleep late at night, or in the grey dawn of morning. They knew how to nurse their vengeance, those two. They stood by patiently, and watched the happiness of the little family—child of Brahma! month of the holy cow! But they were happy and beautiful and good.

"But one day when the prince may have been, in age, two years or thereabouts, he was missed. They never found him. I think the king's grief carried away some of his reason—it sometimes happens so, you know—for when Hari sent him a faqir to tell him that the gods had punished him for being so happy and foretasting heaven on earth, and that he must atone by becoming a Sadhu himself, he objected not, but listened calmly and obeyed.

"'Farewell, beloved!' he said to his little Achthar as he kissed her in her sleep; 'if I love you more than the rest of humanity I am accursed. Farewell!' And drawing his pink garment about him, he took his staff in his hand and walked forth alone. He lives now, they say, in a cave among the far mountains, and pilgrims bless him and travel long ways to look upon his face.

"Rukhi confessed afterwards that they had had the boy conveyed to a lion's den in Kathiawad. He was so small, they must at first, those lions, have fancied him a little cub. But Rukhi is mad, and has a devil—who would punish Rukhi?

"Achthar? Yes, I will tell you. She disappeared soon after these sad things happened. If you ask the villagers here, they will tell you that the gods have made a star of her—that bright little one which is seen about Ganesh Chathurthi, over the highest tower of the palace. But the other side of the valley, near Futeesingh's Mountain, there is a curious little hollow over against a bubbling spring. It is always green and pleasant; pretty ferns grow round about it, and the sacred tulsi, and many sweet-smelling flowers, and great leafy trees hide it from the common gaze. Nothing hinders your going to see it, if you will; nothing, except that there dwells a spirit—a beautiful creature, clothed always in white, of some soft material bordered with gold, like Achthar's famous bridal garb, you know.

"One saw her once, and told us. At nightfall she carries a lamp out on to a stone just outside the hollow, and, with her face to the mountain, she prays till dawn breaks. Futeesingh will be greater than Brahma when he dies—for who prayed like that for Brahma?"

Yes! Achthar knows the hermit, but she will not rob him of his merit as a Sadhu by claiming any particular bit of that which belongs to humanity in general. Herein is love!

Pundit-je

A Portrait

My introduction to the pundit-je was in the autumn, and over things material. He was spiritual and temporal director to our landlord, an infant of years unknown, and he had come to receive the monthly *seignior-age*, and to estimate the probable figure of the repairs-budget, after the heavy monsoon.

I walked round the house and garden with him. "Get this ceiling opened and stretched, pundit-je;" "Cover in this verandah," "Remake that wall," "Mend the sink,"—so I pleaded on our journey; pausing to point out bulging cloth, or shelterless discomfort, or white-ant riddled nuisance: and to each request he would courteously reply, "Certainly, presence! in this matter there can be no question. I live to please you." And emboldened, I begged further. "Just this drain, or that broken railing,"—each versicle winning the most courteous of compliant responses, till—I came to the mango trees! They stretched unwieldy arms across the drive, to the exclusion of all fresh air, and to the very serious damage of carriage hood or human head. On this subject he would not even attempt conciliation.

"No, presence! I *dare* not: the tree would cry aloud if the axe were placed to its fruit-yielding branch. Know you not that these dumb creatures live? Perchance, some friend of a previous birth struggles through this form to higher genesis!"

"Of delicate sensibility art thou, oh pundit-je," said I, somewhat sulkily, "and yet carest nothing that that tree doth offend against my carriage, and my head, and my health!"

"Ah! but," he replied, "the presence has a voice and reason, and can make her own bargains with the Creator, or with fate: that tree looks to me alone for protection."

His answer amused me; and thereafter, every month was the punctual visitor invited to exchange ideas as well as cheques and receipt-stamps.

About the tree, I may mention that I had my way, armed with some municipal order about "cutting down the jungle" (which did not of course apply!); and he treated the inevitable with the dignity reserved for one's bitterest enemy. "Does the presence give me leave to speak?"

he asked. "Then let me quote this wisdom of the wise. To three things submit—*Death, detection, desertion!* Tane-Mahuta (the forest god) knows how to avenge himself. Can I engraft again the branch which the huzoor has severed?"

I would I could make you see him—the spare little man, every line and feature of the keen, clear-cut face bewraying the ascetic and the scholar. *Epigraphic* was he of the East—the old East of the Vedas and priests; and there was in his bearing that consciousness of mental and spiritual superiority which is not incompatible with gentleness, and finds its true expression in ease rather than in assertiveness. And he was well-mannered, to the smallest gesture and detail: the firm, sunburnt feet always shoeless in my presence, and the wisp of grey hair carefully concealed under the accustomed cap or turban. Between the cringing obsequiousness and hybrid disarray of the westernized babu and the dignified courtesy and soft muslin draperies of the old Indian is indeed a great gulf fixed.

He told me that, after his duties as special chaplain to his patron were over, it was his wont to stand or sit in the market-place, and discourse of things philosophical, or expound the Vedas to the temple-goers. Of a quaint, shrewd, classic philosophy, in truth, he possessed a store to envy; and I doubt if all the lessons were learnt in the Sanskrit text.

Methinks he'd seen "the native tints." in every wise "of God's enamel!" Very enjoyable were his morning talks. Fragments of them linger with me still—though, alas! they lose by translation.

On a man raised to sudden power, and overbalanced, he said—

"It is a pity. He forgets our Sanskrit aphorism: 'When you are elevated, and all things are well with you, look above you; there will you find others worthier praise. When depressed, and all things have been ill with you, look below, that you may remember there are others worse off.'"

On another occasion we had been discussing the East, and that official and commercial West which was all that he could see at this distance.

"There was, once," he said, "much wisdom in the East, but it died with men. We have not yet learnt the commerce of thought. 'Times' debtors,' did you say, 'to give back to the world at least our inheritance?' Perhaps, but I go further. We are also, say I, time's *bill-collectors*, and his clients are not only the human but the brute creation.

"Look at the lion. From him must we learn fearlessness, and the power of strength and superiority.

"From the crane, devotion to the moment's duty. Have you watched a crane pick a worm off the ground? No other worm but the one on which it has fixed its desire is allowed to attract its attention—crawl it never so temptingly. It waits and watches, and then—pounce!—the insect has disappeared. *No worm is too small for the exercise of all its faculties.*

"From the dog we might gather a trinity of virtues—

"1. Loyalty to our patrons and friends.

"2. The service of loyalty.

"3. Contentment and cheerfulness.

"Have you never fed a stray dog and noticed his gratitude? And if, next day, you have no bone for him, he will go cheerfully to seek his own meal—coming again to you, however, on the morrow, in unshaken trust."

On the South African war, and the treachery of the Boers, he said, "The English have made, and always make, one great mistake: they trust an enemy! Trust is good, but not for warriors: to 'turn the other cheek' is good, but not for the fighter.

"*The saint* may give good for evil, must forgive, must bless enemies as well as friends, must trust all: *the king* must trust no one!—must smite much, where he is smitten little; may render good for good (*unless his interests require otherwise!*), but must never fail to render evil for evil a thousandfold. And on no pretext should he ever break bread in the house of an enemy, or suffer that enemy to drink even a cup of cold water in his house.

"To the foe, implacability!

"To the friend, a guarded amiability!

"How else should his kingdom stand?"

On Akbar and the reason why he befriended both Hindus and Mohammedans, he was very entertaining.

"Akbar in his first birth was a Hindu *jogi*. Being one day athirst, he asked his palanquin-bearer to bring him a draught of milk. In the heat of the moment he drank the milk *unskimmed*. Now, this to a Hindu is profanation. Said he, 'I am defiled; my next incarnation will be as a Mohammedan—just penance for mine offences. So saying, he lay down and died. He was born again as Akbar, and, bringing with him the remembrance of his Hinduism, was always tolerant of and respectful to the devotees of the cow!"

The pundit-je was rather chary of retailing *superstitions*, but one delightful novelty I did glean from him. "After making a bed, sit on it," he said; "for the devil comes to a bed unoccupied!" No doubt! Are there not other vacuities which he seemeth not loth to fill?

One morning I said to him, "Pundit-je, administer spiritual reproof to such a one of the servants: he is of your religion, and will anger me by telling the most brainless of lies."

"But," said he, "this is the *Kali Yog*, when, for good reason, lies are permissible! The age of *enlightened lying*. If his lies were 'brainless,' certainly he was wrong. But, to save a life, to keep faith, to humour an idiosyncrasy, to raise a laugh, to defraud an enemy, to punish evil-doers—a man may lie!

"The age of uncompromising truth is in the distant past. 'Twas the first or *golden age*."

This opportunist credo of modern days should delight the cynic, read side by side with an extract from the *Brahmanas* (Satapatha Bra. II. ii. 2, 19):

"Whosoever speaks the truth, makes the fire on his own altar blaze up, as if he poured butter into the lighted fire. His own light grows larger, and from to-morrow to to-morrow he becomes better. But whosoever speaks untruth, he quenches the fire on his altar, as if he poured water into the lighted fire; his own light grows smaller and smaller, and from tomorrow to tomorrow he becomes more wicked. Let man therefore speak truth only."

Oh! interpreter of the Vedas! many mighty and many learned in every nation have found it hard to keep "the larger equipoise." Few state their views so fearlessly.

To you, for many a half-hour of quaint refreshment and humour, am I indebted; and I mean to make my debt still heavier!—

Numuscar!

A Note About the Author

Cornelia Sorabji (1866–1954) was an Indian writer, lawyer, and social reformer. Born to Reverend Sorabji Karsdji and Francina Ford, prominent Christian missionaries and converts from Hinduism, Sorabji was raised in Belgaum and Pune. Educated in mission schools and at home, she became the first female graduate of Bombay University before travelling to England in 1889. In 1892, she became the first woman ever to take the Bachelor of Civil Law exam at Oxford University. Sorabji returned to India in 1894 to work as a lawyer representing *purdahnashins*, women barred from communicating with the outside world. Over the course of her decades-long career, Sorabji assisted over 600 women and orphans with their legal needs, often for free. She was also a successful author of articles, books, and such short story collections as *Love and Life Behind the Purdah* (1901). A staunch opponent of Mahama Gandhi's campaign of civil disobedience for Indian self-rule, Sorabji was a controversial figure who stood at the crossroads of the British Raj and the modern Republic of India.

A Note from the Publisher

Spanning many genres, from non-fiction essays to literature classics to children's books and lyric poetry, Mint Edition books showcase the master works of our time in a modern new package. The text is freshly typeset, is clean and easy to read, and features a new note about the author in each volume. Many books also include exclusive new introductory material. Every book boasts a striking new cover, which makes it as appropriate for collecting as it is for gift giving. Mint Edition books are only printed when a reader orders them, so natural resources are not wasted. We're proud that our books are never manufactured in excess and exist only in the exact quantity they need to be read and enjoyed.

Discover more of your favorite classics with Bookfinity™.

- Track your reading with custom book lists.
- Get great book recommendations for your personalized Reader Type.
- Add reviews for your favorite books.
- AND MUCH MORE!

Visit **bookfinity.com** and take the fun Reader Type quiz to get started.

Enjoy our classic and modern companion pairings!

Milton Keynes UK
Ingram Content Group UK Ltd.
UKHW040624231124
451596UK00015B/115

9 781513 280141